The Lifeguard

Katharina Hacker

The Lifeguard

TRANSLATED BY
Helen Atkins

The Toby Press

First Published in German as *Der Bademeister,* 2000, Suhrkamp Verlag

First English language Edition, 2002

The Toby Press *LLC*
www.tobypress.com

ISBN 1 902881 45 1, *hardcover*
ISBN 1 902881 49 4, *paperback*

A CIP catalogue record for this title is available from the British Library

Designed by Breton Jones, London

Original cover photography by Robert Wheeler

Typeset in Garamond by Rowland Phototypesetting Ltd.,
Bury St Edmunds, Suffolk, England

Printed and bound in the United States by
Thomson-Shore Inc., Michigan

Animals answer to their names. Just like people.

Ludwig Wittgenstein,
"Vermischte Bemerkungen" 1948

Chapter one

I'm the lifeguard, and I've never been one to say much. The Swimming Baths are closed. For weeks now the building has been standing empty.

Danger of collapse! At the entrance to the pool area there's a notice. *Danger of collapse. Keep out!*

A slab of plaster broke away from the wall. The caretaker acted quickly. In no time at all the Buildings Inspectorate had been informed so that the stability of the pool hall and the pool itself could be checked. The surveyors who came saw at once that the decay was unstoppable and that there had been subsidence under the pool.

I've never been one to say much, but when it comes to the Swimming Baths I know more than anyone else. I've spent my whole life here.

Don't be misled by the present condition of the baths.

The very first sign of decay was used to justify closing the place down. Because the decision was taken in autumn, just before the onset of winter, rapid deterioration followed. An unheated building is prone to damp, and walls that were previously sound start to develop mould. If I hadn't kept the boilers going for the past three weeks the pipes, which still have water in them, might well have frozen and burst. Flooding would affect first the pool area and then the basement, where it would wreck the heating system. Water would pour out on to the street. The consequences of a flood are incalculable.

It's my responsibility to see that no one drowns. There has to be a clear demarcation between the deeper part of the pool and the shallow area for non-swimmers.

A slab of plaster had broken away from the wall just above the tiling, so the condition of the building and the stability of the pool itself had to be checked. It's not for me to question the findings of the survey. A lifeguard is responsible for the safety of the bathers and the quality of the water. Not that I'm complaining that I was prevented from keeping the water in good condition. I couldn't block the decisions that were taken, and I drained the pool myself.

I never said much, no one could expect me to, but anything that was necessary I said loud and clear. *Warning to non-swimmers! The deepest part of the pool is three meters deep!*

To a disinterested observer the Public Baths and Swimming Pool may look like an old or even obsolete building. It's almost a hundred years old, it opened at the beginning of the century, and in the early years it was used by some three thousand people each week. The heating system was renewed fifteen years ago, and although the boilers are still coal-fired, the air and water temperatures have always been comfortable. Only a malicious person would claim that the swimming pool has become run down. While I wouldn't deny its shortcomings, these are outweighed by the special merits of the architecture and interior detailing.

I'm assuming that you are free of any such malice. I've

never been one to say much, and throughout my working life I've made it my rule to employ the strictest reserve. But now it has become necessary to breach that reserve. For weeks, as I can testify, no one has paid any attention to the needs of the swimming pool. As I have reason to suppose that you can hear me, I will describe its condition to you. Even though I've no legal right to be here, you can't question my competence to speak on these matters. I'm the lifeguard; I've spent my whole life here.

Various attempts have been made to slander me. It's unfair. I've never been one to talk much, and if I'm in the habit of talking to myself, then it's my own business. No one has ever drowned. I have just spent weeks sitting in silence in the pool area looking at the pool. A thin layer of dust has settled on the tiles, blackish dust marked by my footprints. From the edge one can see clearly where I've gone down the steps and walked through the shallow end and then the whole length of the pool. The oblong turquoise tiles are laid in a staggered pattern; under the water the deliberate variation in their coloring used to create the impression of a natural pond or lake. Now the colors are smothered by the dust, reduced to a dull gray relieved only by my footprints. This pool has been in existence for almost a hundred years, and for all those years the tiles survived intact. The grouting material was resistant to water but is affected by exposure to the air and dust, and so the tiles are coming loose, rattling when you walk on them, and cracking. You need to know all these details. If something isn't done soon the decay will be irreversible.

This morning a second slab of plaster broke away from the wall. I heard the sound it made. The first time this happened, some weeks ago, I had just gone out for a moment and the caretaker was alone in the pool area. I no longer believe this to have been a mere coincidence.

First there was an impact, then the sound of fragments

spattering in all directions. It was not unlike the sound of some large, flat object hitting the water. But the pool is empty.

As I ran to the spot I saw again, out of the corner of my eye, some movement up in the gallery. I don't know what it signifies, but strange things are happening here. All my life I've kept my eye on everything and taken care that no one should drown. Now I get fleeting glimpses of figures moving about up there, and sometimes around the pool too, as if the bathers had come back. I'm not happy about this, because when I call out to them there's no reply. There they sit, up in the gallery on the high-backed wooden seats, leaning expectantly over the rail as though they were watching me. The pool hall is dim; I daren't turn on the lights, and the glass bricks in the arch at the back end are dirty, like the panes of milky glass in the basement boiler room. Even in the daytime it doesn't get really light any more. The ground under the building is giving way, subsiding, and the pool gradually sinking.

That's what the inspection revealed, and so I had to drain the pool. I did so without protest, although the surveyors who came to carry out the safety check spent a long time in the office with the manageress, Frau Karpfe, and only took a cursory look at the pool area. I have known this area for almost forty years and have not noticed anything that could be seen with the naked eye. I still don't believe that the pool had already been subsiding. It's only very recently that any change has been visible. The ground is subsiding, and the building with it.

I have always believed that errors and irregularities would come to light of their own accord. But the years went by and no lifeguard was appointed. I never wanted to be a lifeguard, I had other plans. I would only have to stay until a new lifeguard was found, they informed me. In all those years I never mentioned it.

I have reason to believe that you can hear me.

When I heard the sound today I realized at once what had made it. I ran over and saw the slab of plaster and paint, as large as two heads, and a gaping hole in the wall above the pillar. As on the first occasion, it was just above one of the pillars, where the wall isn't tiled, where there's a small projection separating the pillar from the arch. I remembered how the previous time the caretaker had cleared away the mess, although normally he never touched anything with his own hands but always summoned me or one of the cleaning women when there was any dirt to be got rid of. Just for a moment I hadn't been in the pool hall but had gone down to the boiler room to give Klaus a towel that a swimmer had left behind, as the lost property cupboard is in the basement. While I was waiting for Klaus to clean the coal dust off his hands, I looked at his two aquariums and saw that in the larger one there were now only six fishes swimming about. I ate one yesterday, Klaus said with a grin when he noticed me looking at them. Pity they're not *Karpfe*— carp—he said. This was a dig at the manageress, Frau Karpfe— he never did like her, nor the caretaker. They're informers, both of them, I tell you; they've still got the place bugged. They sit in the office listening to what people are saying in the pool area, you ought to be more careful.

But I've never had anything to hide. Why should they do that, I would answer Klaus each time. But now I've seen that above the pillars the wall is a different color, as if someone had tampered with it, and twice a slab of plaster has come away just there.

I learned, through years of practice, to see not only what I was looking at directly but also whatever was going on around the periphery. You can't watch thirty swimmers at once and keep in view a twenty-meter long pool unless you learn to pick up the slightest movement at the blurred edges of your vision. I would walk around the pool, confidently and without stumbling, and out of the corner of my eye I could see even the entrances to the changing rooms, and the gallery too. Now I find that my own feet intrude into the picture, and this is part of the general disorder that is taking hold. In the past I wore beach sandals and only rarely put on my white trainers, early in the morning or in the evening when there were no swimmers left in the water. Now the trainers are gray and covered with black smudges from the coal dust in the basement, and the left one has a burn-hole, just below my ankle, made by a spark from the boiler. I often look down and follow the line of red tiles that warns you to keep back from the edge of the pool, and so I lose sight of the pool itself and the gallery and am only vaguely conscious of some movement up there, but when I call there's no reply.

Since this morning I've been circling the pool again, walking slowly from one pillar to the next, hesitantly because I'm out of practice. For the first three weeks after losing my job I just wandered around the city. I started murmuring to myself again, and the children laughed at me just as they had done in the past. Look at him; he's talking to himself, a boy said loudly. They followed me for a short distance, and passers-by turned to look at me. You can't really blame children for behaving like that. But those other people told deliberate lies about me. The caretaker never liked me. He thinks he's a cut above the rest of us, he said. He's mad, he talks to himself. I had never done him any harm. Who else was there for me to talk to?

When I approach his kiosk, Cremer greets me in a friendly way. Good morning, Hugo. Good evening, Hugo. Then he relapses into silence, or else he reads out an item from a newspaper. At one time we used to talk about his daughter Tanja.

"Have you read this?" he asks, though he knows I don't read a paper, and he starts to read it out to me. I haven't seen him since my mother's death.

"You should be glad you've lost your job. High time you

got out of there. You can start reading books again," he said, although I'd told him how my mother boxed up my books years ago.

"They're just dust-collectors," she claimed, and I had to carry them down to the street myself. As for the warning notices and rules posted up at the Swimming Baths, I've known them by heart for a long time now.

I have maintained this silence for years. That's over now. You can tell by listening to me that I'm not crazy. Since I've been waiting for that sound, the silence has been unbearable. Even in the semi-darkness the gaping hole in the wall is visible.

For three weeks I just wandered around the city. I have every right to be here. Where else should I go?

I had the key to the side entrance. A narrow, low-ceilinged passage leads from there to the boiler room. I'd never used it before. When I entered the pool hall for the first time in weeks I remained standing by the steps as though I were rooted to the spot, staring at the pool in the half-light. I heard voices, voices and splashing, and saw bathers lowering themselves, one after another, into the water. They didn't resurface. Frightened, I ran to the edge of the pool, stood there with my arms outstretched, tried to call out all the things that a lifeguard must call out to avert disaster, but the phrases sounded strange and ridiculous. For a moment I thought I had been mistaken, and that there were big, hollow plastic dolls floating on the water, but then three children detached themselves from the wall, giggling, raced each other to the side of the pool and jumped in, although jumping in from the sides is prohibited. Do you hear what I'm saying? Someone's playing tricks on me, trying to make a fool of me. But I'm not having it. I have total recall of all that has happened.

For all those years I watched people coming and going and didn't know their names. I didn't want to know, and never tried to get into conversation with them. No one has drowned, in my whole life, and I have not harmed anyone.

If there are microphones here, they must be concealed at the point where the pillars meet the arches. A small projection separates the lower, tiled part from the plastered wall above. The walls are painted a bright yellow, which has faded, but above the pillars one can see a slight difference in color. You can't fool me. If I go and stand in the middle of the empty pool and speak softly you won't hear a word. People have noticed that I talk to myself. Even if it's true, it can't be held against me. There's no rule against it.

All my life I have worked and done what I was ordered to do. After a few years you come to understand what really matters. No one knows the baths as well as I do.

Klaus set up two aquariums in the basement. He claimed that a swimming pool ought to have fish, and that he was bored. Nothing but coal all day long, the dust and the stink of it, for ten hours or more, because Frau Karpfe had appointed just him on his own when she was supposed to take on two boiler men. She did the same with me. A new lifeguard would replace the old one, whose assistant I was, that was the story to begin with, and later they promised that a second lifeguard would share the work with me, because I was on duty fourteen hours a day here, from seven in the morning to nine at night. I never said anything about it. Perhaps Frau Karpfe pocketed the two wages herself, or shared them with the caretaker.

When he reported to her that Klaus was keeping fish, she threatened to give Klaus his notice but did nothing about it. She had more sense: Klaus worked weekends and was doing the work of two men anyway. From the moment he started working at the public baths he hardly ever set foot outside them. It wasn't right. He made no attempt to conceal the fish. Not long before the baths were closed down he came with a bucket to scoop some water out of the pool. For my catfish, he said with a grin. You can eat catfish. In the tool store he opened the safety valves and cooked using the hot steam. I don't care if it's against the rules, he said loudly. The catfish are still alive although they went for weeks without being fed. Perhaps it was something about the water from the pool, or else they fed on each other. Now they're in a bad way. They swim about very slowly, as if they're ill, as if they know it will all be over soon. They've grown very big since I've been back, and their black whiskers trail along the bottom. They look like fishes of death, and if they were to die that would be a bad omen. I don't know much about fish. It's not my fault. I was only responsible for the pool area, for seeing that nobody drowned. The instruction notices are positioned so as to be clearly visible:

Take care when using the pool step-ladders!
Face towards the steps!
Jumping in from the sides is strictly prohibited!

And I was never ill, although I did the work of two men for almost forty years. Frau Karpfe and the caretaker can confirm that. Whatever I could do, I did. Look at the pool now—there's a layer of dust covering the tiles, the colors look dull and faded. At night you can hear mice squeaking, and I've seen rats too. The water in the changing rooms has been cut off, the shower heads hang there like metal ghosts, like gaunt bird-heads stuck on spikes. Dirt on the tiles; benches and coat-stands missing, that whole area plundered and bare—like an abattoir, just about good enough for animal carcasses, with drainage gullies for the blood. There's a putrid smell coming from the taps, and at night the rats are busy here, they can't wait for me to leave too so that there's no one left to disturb them. Is that what you're waiting for? For a reason to pull down the whole building?

But I'm not going to keep quiet about it any longer.

There must be some mistake. The Public Baths and

The Lifeguard

Swimming Pool has existed since the turn of the century. The gallery extends around three sides. Two broad arches support five narrower ones, between which the spectators sit on high-backed wooden benches. At the front the gallery is supported by stone lintels adorned with lion heads, which have menacingly raised paws and sharp claws. Do you hear me? I know these Swimming Baths inside out. Somebody has to watch over the building. The banisters on the stairs leading down to the basement and the ones in the entrance hall are of wrought iron, adorned with fat little fish. Upstairs, there are the bathtubs inside cubicles, where people can take a bath. When the public baths were first opened, some three thousand people would come here each week. It can't be true: a whole baths complex can't be shut down just like that. I'm only fifty-eight. I could easily go on working for another ten years. They wouldn't need to appoint a second lifeguard. If I could only switch on the big lights above the pool that would make all the difference. You can't see clearly in the half-light. I walk around the pool as though I still needed to ensure that no one drowns. *Jumping in from the sides is strictly prohibited!* Up on the gallery and along the sides of the pool, I can see them. They're moving quickly or else standing quite rigid, I can't make them out clearly. When I call, they don't answer. I have called out loudly, thinking that I was mistaken, that they were not really there. But they keep reappearing, moving as if they were ill or feeling cold. I won't let them make a fool of me. They must answer! Either they don't notice me or they're pretending they can't hear me. I'm speaking loudly enough. They are the bathers who used to come, and now I feel sorry that I never knew their names. Can you hear me? My name's Hugo.

Now that that sound may recur at any time; I can't bear the silence. Every sound signifies further decay. Soon no one will remember how it used to be. There are two notices missing.

The warnings are inadequate. I've never understood why people swim, but while I've been here no one has drowned. Now there'd have to be a notice saying: *Warning! Anyone who swims is liable to drown!*

No one could check whether that's true or not. *Face towards the pool steps!* One of the step-ladders is missing, and the other two no longer reach the bottom. The pool, the whole building is sinking, as though there were a hollow space under the city, and the clock has stopped.

It's so quiet. The whole place used to echo with shouting and splashing, as though water were a cause for rejoicing. I could never understand that. Sometimes I lowered the temperature by three or four degrees. Then the adults would give a start of surprise, shiver and swim in silence, while the children simply didn't notice and went on laughing and shouting. Noise and splashing, day in, day out. I never wanted to be a lifeguard. Now it's quiet, I can see my own feet in their trainers, the empty pool, a swimming pool without water, a lifeguard without a pool, and it's worse than a person drowning, it's an abomination, like the soot-blackened trainers—I would never have let anyone in wearing those—and I often stumble. I can't say exactly how much time has passed. It can't be measured any more, it drags on so slowly, and a day is so long that you can't think as far as the end of it, it's as long as weeks used to be. Time is accumulating like water that can't drain away, the whole pool is already full of it. The most basic divisions become blurred, not even the tiles can be counted, they're covered with a black layer of dirt, dust that has become damp here and there, and only the grimacing lion heads are unchanged, possibly with microphones hidden in their mouths, perhaps someone's eavesdropping on me, waiting for the chance to betray me. Anxiously, I listen out for the door, whether it's being unlocked and footsteps are approaching, whether someone's coming to turn me out. You must prevent that happening. If I am forced to go, there'll be nobody left here.

For three weeks I wandered around the city. I can't say for certain how much time has passed since I came back here. Time shifts imperceptibly from one twilight to another, it never gets really light, or really dark either because of the light from the street lamps. The days merge into each other as though they were a single day and time were nothing but decay, rust eating away at the pipes and iron struts, lumps falling out of the wall, dust forming a dry layer or becoming damp and slimy. I keep the boilers going, but the coal is running out and soon I will be unable to stop the pipes from freezing and bursting. There's no boiler man here now. Klaus has gone away, along with the others, but he left the fish behind. Sometimes I think it's always been like this, the Swimming Baths derelict, the pool empty, and in the emptiness around it nothing but my own voice. In the corridor between the entrance hall and the pool area the big mirror is still in place, and as I pass it I see little more than a shadow, a shadow like any other, a sunken face, eyes too deep-set, only the nose still jutting out sharply; the soiled clothes hang loosely on the body, which looks cowed and shrinks back hesitantly, then hurries on; a stranger isn't allowed to enter the pool area in such a state. At the start I made it a strict rule to take a shower and put on a clean shirt every day. But now I don't leave the Swimming Baths any more, and I have no clean clothes to change into.

It started when I was wandering around the city. Even Cremer wouldn't have recognized me in the street. First there's the smell, a smell of weariness and fear, and soon it's as if the body harbored decay within it and were a foreign body among the other passers-by, among people who have a reason to hurry as they go to work, as they go home. I felt as if I was an alien presence among all those who know exactly where they're going;

a weary body slowly collapsing, emitting a nasty smell, first it's at other people's knee height, then the face is alongside coat hems and trouser legs, and finally the eyes are on a level with shoes, warm winter shoes with thick soles.

It's the clothes that show the first signs. You can't keep them clean any more, the smell clings to them, and soon the soles of your shoes are worn down, the uppers are scuffed because your feet stumble, and your jacket rubs thin on the walls of buildings, your trousers pick up the dirt from steps and railings because you have to lean on something, you can't keep going non-stop, and your face is puffy as though it were trying, out of shame, to become unrecognizable. It's not long before children start staring at you and adults look away and move on quickly as if they were afraid of catching something. You attract attention, you walk aimlessly but as though you were in a great hurry, and even time loses its direction, you go round in circles, keep coming back to the same morning, take the same route again, try to walk the day away, and then the day starts all over again.

If I come back here, everything will return to normal— that's what I thought. Time has its fixed place, there's a big clock below the lion heads, below the pillars supporting the seating.

When the pool hall was empty you could hear the clock ticking in the silence. But now it's stopped, and instead of the ticking you hear only the rats and mice or a slab of plaster and paint breaking away from the wall, shattering on the floor. It happened this morning. The silence attaches itself to the walls like a leech, and nothing remains of time—just sounds of decay and gradual destruction. When I hear a soft rustling I don't know if it's mortar trickling from the wall, or the mice. I've searched in the boiler room for traps and poison, but without success. There never used to be vermin in the Swimming Baths. I didn't tolerate dirt. Now I can't do anything about it. But the silence, the silence is something I can't endure.

I never counted the bathers. There were large numbers of them, every day, and anyone who denies that is a liar. Only the individual baths were used less than before because nowadays most people have got a bath at home. Now they've all stopped coming, just as though this place had never existed.

"What of it?" Cremer said when he visited me after my mother's death, "They just aren't going swimming any more, or if they are, they're going somewhere else. You of all people," he added, "ought to understand that, after all you've never swum yourself."

But even though he's right, I can't understand why so many people should suddenly stay away as if they hadn't been coming here for years, as if all those years had vanished into thin air as soon as a cardboard notice was hung across the entrance saying: *The swimming pool is closed.*

You're right, I answered. I wanted to say to him, there's nothing left, I wake up in the morning and reach out to take hold of something, a shirt, my shoes, I grope for the light switch and my hand stays empty. I get up in the dark, there's no need, and I don't have to rush. Even first thing in the morning time hangs heavy, all those hours until evening, the people in the street hurrying by as though nothing had happened, as though no one but me knew that the swimming pool has been closed. They managed it very cleverly, I wanted to say to Cremer. *Danger of collapse! Due to subsidence of the pool.* No one objected. Do you hear? Klaus said nothing either. Before he got the job at the baths he was out of work, he told me that himself. What they've promised him I don't know. They're all in cahoots with each other. I haven't seen any of them since. Klaus maintained that the caretaker was an informer. Then from one day to the next he stopped speaking to me. Leave him alone, he's mad, that's what the others said about me.

They must have been hatching some plan from the start,

I told Cremer. The swimming pool is just the beginning. Nonsense, Cremer replied. The swimming pool is closed. That's all there is to it.

I walked through the streets expecting someone to say something, but no one stopped. It was a day just like any other, I left the house at the same time as I did every morning, and if I'd gone the right way I would have been at work on time, though not in the right clothes—no lifeguard stands by the pool in cords and a shirt. But I went in the opposite direction and only arrived at Cremer's kiosk as evening was falling. He waved a greeting to me, but angrily, and held out the paper bag with the two dry cheese rolls that he'd got ready for me that morning.

"What am I supposed to do with them now?" he asked crossly, and where had I been this morning? I took the bag without a word. We said no more to each other that day. Nobody stopped and said, "You're the lifeguard, aren't you? Listen, the baths are closed today; all of a sudden the public baths are shut. Not even the individual baths are in use now."

Cremer had heard nothing about it, he probably thought I was still looking after the bathtubs, and people were stopping to buy their paper just as they would on any other day. Cremer motioned to me to move aside because I was blocking the little window of his kiosk.

I took the bag and went away, and if it had been warm weather I could have sat on a park bench, like a person who really likes eating his supper out of doors. But it was the first day of December. I'd been wandering around the city all day and was chilled to the marrow, but it was too early to go back to the flat, I never got in before nine o'clock. I wrapped one of the rolls in the paper bag and stuffed it into my jacket pocket, and ate the other as I walked along. It was still too early to make for home, and I couldn't go to the baths. I've never eaten in the street, and I thought that anyone looking at me would be able to tell that I had nowhere to go. My mother wasn't expecting me at that hour; she'd have been surprised and would have bombarded me with questions. Aren't you working? Why are you back so early? I told her nothing. Right up to her death she never knew that the Swimming Baths had been closed down.

The fish are really sick, and of the four globes standing next to the aquarium another, a second one, has gone out after flickering for some time. Let's hope it's only the plug, I thought, and checked it, but it's the bulb that's gone. In the boiler room there aren't any bulbs, only a few neon tubes in the tool store. The globe flickered as if to give warning, just as my voice would warn a swimmer who kept on swimming even though he was utterly exhausted, breathing shallowly and staring wide-eyed like someone far out in a lake desperately looking for the shore. I always noticed in time when disaster threatened. After a final flicker the globe went out for good.

Outside it has grown dark, the street lamps have come on, and the dim twilight envelops the empty pool and the tiles, which once shone bright turquoise even in the faintest light but are now fading from sight, dull and without luster, as if the color had been driven out of them; the grotesque lion faces are merging into the shadows under the gallery. If I don't say what is here, everything will disappear, the lion heads, the gallery, the entire building. Only my voice remains to tell what no one can see any more, because the baths are closed, the main entrance door not merely locked but also secured by a chain. Do you hear me? I've never been one to talk much, but now I must name everything, just as you try to retrieve a foreign object from the water with your hand, but finally fetch the net on its long pole, to catch it just before it sinks to the bottom. When anything fell into the pool I always made sure to fish it out quickly before it could get waterlogged and sink, possibly disintegrating or leaving streaks of impurity that could sully the water, which has to be clear. The quality of the water is very important.

Now the pool is empty. At first I tried sweeping it with a broom. But the dust only rises up in a cloud and in no time a new layer has formed. In a few places it's damp; there the dust clings, a black film of dirt, and in the feeble light the appearance is deceptive. The pool looks like a deep chasm. I must take care to ensure that no one jumps in, either from the side or from the diving board, for if anyone did, he'd break his neck, and die without even having drowned. No one has ever drowned here, and jumping in from the side is prohibited.

There would be a great commotion. Screams and cries for help, a doctor, an ambulance. The drowned or nearly-drowned casualty would be carried out on a stretcher, I'd be desperately running to and fro between the dead or potentially dying victim and the pool, which must never be left unsupervised, I would order anyone still swimming to leave the water immediately, and for the rest of my life I'd have to ask myself how it could have happened and why I hadn't prevented it. I always tried to be circumspect and do things right, and in fact I've succeeded. The days passed uniformly and without disturbance, I never needed to give a loud shout, either to warn or to call for help, it was enough to raise my voice, at most to call out; speaking loudly and clearly was enough to avert any threat of danger, so that no untoward event ever occurred. Do you understand: no event ever occurred, I made it my goal to ensure that my life be uneventful, and actually I've succeeded.

They can't touch me. For a whole lifetime I was the lifeguard, and nothing ever happened, the days went by one after another. You have no suspicions or forebodings; I made every effort to see that nothing happened. Only now do I realize that it's been in vain. My dismissal hasn't prevented it, and it rests with others to decide whether anything has happened or not. As long as no one says anything, nothing has taken place. Do *you* know what has happened? The baths have been closed, first the pool and then the cubicles with the bathtubs too. When the last gallon of water had been drained off and the pool was empty— the bathers had been banished three days earlier—I walked along the street on my way home and saw people passing by as though nothing had happened. They don't know, I thought, but when they find out they'll see to it that the baths are re-opened.

The next morning the caretaker was there with a grin for me:

"Have fun looking after the bathtubs!"

Now they've dismissed me for good—I'm not needed even for the bathtubs.

"They've sorted something out," I told Cremer when he asked me what I would do once the pool was drained.

"That's all right, then," he said indifferently, and later I stopped going to his kiosk. It was only when I needed his advice about my dead mother that I told him I'd been dismissed.

When something has happened you just have to get used to it, and before long it's as if nothing had happened at all. A few years back Cremer broke his leg, and since then he's walked with a limp because the bone didn't mend straight. No one ever mentions it, and you might easily think he'd been born that way. It's the same when some object falls into the water: for a short while you see rings on the surface, but soon all is calm again, the water is as motionless as before, and only a person who knows about it may possibly catch sight of an object lying on the bottom. And even then you don't have to fish it out: it's enough just to keep silent.

I have let myself fall prey to an illusion. You think that something has happened, but it hasn't. When someone goes swimming, either he doesn't drown or else he does. Even if he nearly dies, he hasn't actually died, and everything goes on just as usual. An onlooker seeing the danger feels a shock of alarm, but is calm again a moment later. Everything always calms down again in no time at all. People think that the greatest shock would be if the worst happened, but the opposite is true. Even supposing a bather had drowned, things would soon be back to normal again. All it takes is for nobody to talk about it. I might have been dismissed, perhaps, but after just a few days no one would have given it another thought: one bather less, a new lifeguard, a shake of the head or a clasping together of hands, a quick flash of curiosity in the eyes, and that's all. People still stop when the lights turn to red, and if they drop a glove they bend down to pick it up. To suppose that things have changed is an illusion. The days go by, one after another, and nobody says anything, but anyone who goes on insisting that a disaster has occurred finds that time stands still for him and no day ever seems to pass.

The clock has stopped working, and I won't keep quiet. The silence is terrible; the hours, the days, they all grow longer and longer, they lose all sense of direction, like blinded horses walking in a circle to draw water from a well. Cremer read to me about them from a magazine when I told him that I was having to drain the water from the pool. The horses walk round and round a well to raise the buckets of water, and because they can't see it doesn't bother them, Cremer explained, showing me a photograph.

The blinkered horses go round and round, but the pool is already empty, the water has long since been drained. I did it myself, it took three days, and at first there was no noticeable change in the water level, so that although I myself had opened the outlet valve I went back again to check, because the level seemed to stay the same and there wasn't a sound to be heard.

The water flows away quite soundlessly. The horses plod on and on because that's all they know, and even if the well is empty they don't stop and they don't rest, and one day is no different from another.

Because I couldn't see whether the water level was falling, I walked round the pool, circled it, went from one pillar to the next, past the exit under the gallery with the lions, along the length of the pool to the shell-shaped niche under the big glazed arch, and on and on in a circle, past the changing rooms, like a horse, an old nag who from mere force of habit doesn't stop, doesn't die, and even if he were dead would go plodding on, harnessed, blind, just as I am still walking, even now, round the empty pool.

The days I've spent in here alone have passed without a sound, and they seem to stretch into years. Once there were always people here, always voices. I haven't been speaking out loud until now—what was there to say? Instead I murmured quietly to myself, even when I was tired, because I couldn't bear the silence. Time doesn't pass.

Now I don't care if anyone can hear me. I'm not going to wait and say nothing until the public baths are demolished and no instructions remain but: *Go and stand in the middle of the pool. Do not try to shield your head with your hands. Wait for the sound of the wrecker's ball. You need not worry: the roof will be the first thing to collapse.*

I used to stumble a lot when I first started working here. Whenever I had the chance I would slip my rubber sandals off and put trainers on instead. In plastic or wooden sandals it's easy to stumble, you have to learn to use your toes to draw the rest of the foot and the sandal along. But you soon get used to doing this movement while going at a reasonable speed, since you aren't walking far in the sandals, just round the pool.

It was only out in the street that I walked fast, going the

short distance between the flat and the baths, and then, after I had been sacked, all over the city for hours on end. The outdoor shoes that I never used in all my time as a lifeguard are now worn out. As a child I would have been punished for that, for my father expected me to take care of my shoes, and when he hanged himself his shoes, dangling in mid-air, had new soles.

I hardly tolerated my work colleagues to be in the pool area, I didn't want them coming in with their shifty glances, always ready to make fun of someone, waiting to pounce on someone, as perhaps they're still spying on me now. They weren't to be trusted. From her office, Frau Karpfe was able to keep the entrance area under surveillance using a mirror, and she always came up with reasons not to admit anyone she didn't want. But the Public Baths are open to all comers, so she had no right to do that. If she thought of a job for someone she would call for them loudly and impatiently, and a question from her would develop into an interrogation.

"She's having an affair with the caretaker, and he's an informer," Klaus said. Sometimes she would barricade herself away in the office, lock the door and complete silence would reign. At other times she was visited by people who hadn't come to swim or to take a bath, and I saw that she kept a bottle of cognac in her filing cabinet. Then she would let no one but the caretaker into the office. She would have long consultations with him, after which she would roundly declare to all of us to expect repercussions.

"This will have repercussions," she would say, "the individuals concerned will soon see where it gets them." And everyone would nod, because no one knew what she was talking about.

I refuse to let myself be slandered. She used to claim that I was simple-minded, a half-wit, or so Klaus told me; that I was incapable of anything but parroting the words on the notices or asking for chlorine—the caretaker said that to my face. One of these days the chlorine will have completely rotted your brain. Whenever I needed chlorine or flocculent they would insist on my handing in a written request, and then they would always lose it and need another one.

"Good morning," I would say each morning, and nothing more, and it suited me very well if they ignored me and hardly ever came into the pool area.

"Good evening," I would say in the evening, but by then everyone had generally gone. Then I would leave the building through the boiler room in the basement, closing behind me the heavy iron door, which didn't need locking. I suppose the care-taker had forgotten that when he gave me the key to the side entrance, just as he then forgot about the key and didn't ask me to return it. I was usually the last to leave the baths, though sometimes there was still a boiler man down in the basement. Before Klaus came there were two boiler men working alternate shifts, just as there must once have been two lifeguards.

The others left me in peace, only coming into the pool area when it was unavoidable, and the cleaning was done very early in the morning before I arrived. Only on the day when the slab of plaster and paint broke away from the wall did they all gather by the pool, and from that day on the caretaker found some pretext or other to come in every day and look at the walls, the damage, and then me, as if I had open sores on my body. *People with broken skin and rashes are not allowed to use the pool.* They smelled it, they smelled the decay like fish smelling blood, they wanted to see the damage with their own eyes over and over again, and they laughed when they realized how I wished I could ban them from the pool area. The caretaker and the manageress had a plan, do you hear? There is something that they wanted to conceal, even if I don't know exactly what it is. I'm not mad. They listed two boiler men and two lifeguards on the payroll and pocketed the extra wages themselves. Do you hear? You can't keep a swimming bath open for fourteen hours a day with just one boiler man and one lifeguard. But I never wanted to become a lifeguard, and it was all the same to me how many hours I spent here every day. There was never any way out of it.

For three weeks I wandered around the city. My mother had no idea that I was unemployed. She despised my job—a lifeguard, what sort of a job is that, she would say indignantly. After the Wall fell she expected that at last I would take up some other kind of work. I was almost fifty. Every evening she'd be there, waiting at the door to ask me if I'd done anything about it. I stayed at the baths until nine o'clock at night and took my time changing so as not to get home before half past nine. She went to bed early. We hardly exchanged a word.

Days spent in a flat are too long. You go up and down the hallway and from one room to another. She never worked. And then a few weeks ago she died.

Nobody is going to drive me out of here. I will not wander around the city again. I've done nothing wrong, and I will not go back to wandering around the city until I can't move another step and have to rest on park benches and at bus stops because I'm exhausted, and anyway I'm only going round in circles and getting lost. I've seen people rummaging in dustbins and people lying, eyes closed, with chapped hands, out in the cold in archways and on the front steps of shops, until they get moved on; they have a bad smell clinging to their clothes and bodies. I'm not going to let that happen to me again. I was aware of that smell, my own smell of sweat, street dirt and fear. In here, although I miss the smell of water and chlorine, it's still better than having that bad smell, which other people notice before you do yourself. Now my clothes are dirty because I'm dealing with the boilers. The smell of coal penetrates right into your skin. I don't shower every day now, it doesn't do any good. If

I don't run the heating here the pipes will freeze. Do you want to see the building collapse?

When my mother died I went to see Cremer. At first he was offended that I had kept away for so long, but then he came with me to the flat to help. I didn't know what one normally does in such cases, because after my father hanged himself the police came round. Cremer phoned an undertaker's, and two hours later their man was ringing at the door. I didn't want to go to the cemetery, I said, and he suggested that I could have her laid to rest as an unnamed urn, an unnamed urn without a ceremony, he explained, that would be the cheapest way of doing it. Cremer was outraged. It wasn't as if the ground was frozen, he said, like when the ground had had to be specially broken up with pneumatic drills for his mother. But I hadn't attended my father's funeral, and I didn't want to go to my mother's. She outlived him by forty years. It's nothing to do with me.

Here I sleep in the basement on an old camp bed that Klaus put up for his own use and left behind. I lie stretched out on my back, quite straight and without any covering, because it's warm in the basement, there's no danger of being cold. I lie there stretched out, feet together, arms crossed so that my head rests on my forearms. Just the way a dead person might lie, it occurred to me yesterday, and now I don't like lying there any more. There are churches where real dead bodies are placed on view in glass coffins; Cremer read it to me from a magazine.

For the first few years I hated the Swimming Baths as though I were buried there. Now the pool is empty, and it would make a good cemetery, a place for dead bodies where bathers once used to swim. No one has ever come to harm through any fault of mine, and no one has drowned while I've been the lifeguard.

At the start I hated working here, hated the noise, the boredom, but later I enjoyed the work. I spent more time here

than was originally intended, because I was left doing the work
for which two people were supposed to be employed, and I
didn't mind that. Where was my colleague, people asked me,
the old lifeguard whose assistant I had been, where had he disappeared to? I had better think carefully about that, I was told,
since as long as it slipped my mind I'd find myself having to
stay here.

"Didn't he tell you anything at all?" asked the man who
was the manager at that time sneeringly. Then he tapped his
desk impatiently, "Take your time to think about it," I was
advised, "after all, you're not short of time here."

And I did have plenty of time, all the time in the world,
until nothing was left of the world and of my plans. They've
probably forgotten about you, the manager remarked indifferently. Then he was replaced, so was the caretaker, and I was the
only one still here when Frau Karpfe came.

"I take it you don't want any trouble?" she asked me.
"We shall be keeping an eye on you."

They never appointed a second lifeguard, or an assistant;
the manageress tacitly assumed that I would cover all the hours
by myself, opening up the baths early in the morning, closing
them late in the evening and never taking any holidays. I had
started out as the lifeguard's assistant, not even as a proper
apprentice; I used to leave as early as I could, and I went to the
baths reluctantly and was glad to get away again. I never wanted
to be a lifeguard. It had to have been some mistake that I was
prevented from going to university, I thought as I continued to
read my books at home, just a temporary mistake: as soon as I'd
proved my reliability I would be released, and until then I would
just have to persevere. I had all the time in the world, and
eventually people stopped being surprised that I was doing the
work of two. Only when I was dismissed did Frau Karpfe say
in a threatening tone that I had done overtime, voluntarily, she

said with strong emphasis, and I had no claim to payment for it, she added, as though I intended to rob her.

I had plenty of time. I thought of this again when, on returning to the baths, I walked around inside the building and came upon the cobwebs on the back stairs leading to the gallery and the bath cubicles. This staircase was hardly ever used and the spiders could operate undisturbed, for even when the pool hall was painted, the workmen sometimes overlooked that narrow stairway. I discovered it when I first started working here, the old lifeguard insisted on my getting to know every nook and cranny of the building. I brushed them away with my hand, and I remember how soft they were to the touch, disgustingly so because you felt you wanted to sweep away the mass of web with all your strength. I only touched it that once, and I was left with threads sticking to my hand and to my hair as if it were my head that had brushed up against them. Now there are cobwebs everywhere, on the underside of the gallery, in every corridor and in the changing rooms. Even in the pool they're gradually spreading along the handrails, and I've stopped trying to remove them.

I didn't tell Cremer straight away that I'd lost my job. On the following day, when I only came to his kiosk in the evening and he angrily gave me the two rolls, I merely said that I wouldn't be needing any rolls for the next day's lunch. Because there were other customers waiting to buy newspapers, he just motioned to me to move aside out of their way and I said goodbye and went off. But for my mother's death, he wouldn't know to this day that the Baths had been closed and I'd lost my job. What had I been doing all that time since it happened, he wanted to know, but I couldn't tell him. It's so quiet suddenly, I said. You wake up in the morning, I wanted to explain, and you turn round and you can't see where you've come from. Then you start going round in circles. You go round in circles because you don't know where to go. There ought to be something in your head, I wanted to say to him, that explains how it's all come about. But all that time has vanished. There's not even a notice to warn you about it. I wake up in the morning and know I haven't enough breath to get up, I'm panting and as out of breath as if I'd spent the whole night running in my sleep, and when I want to say something I'm too short of breath to speak. I wanted to explain to him that I wake up and don't recognize anything, not even the room where I've slept since I was a child. It's as though you'd suddenly gone blind, I wanted to tell him, and forgotten how everything used to look.

"The buildings, the cars, even the people look different from before," I replied to Cremer's question, "nobody goes to the baths any more. Maybe the people are the same, but I only know them undressed, I find all the clothes confusing."

"You're talking nonsense," Cremer said, shaking his head anxiously. "Your mother was quite old," he said to comfort me, thinking I was in a confused state because of my mother's death. He had come to the flat at my request, and after the undertaker's man had gone he sat down with me in the living room, where I hadn't sat for years. There's a coffee table flanked by a floral-patterned sofa and two armchairs, and beyond it is a television set. The low, glass-fronted cupboard is empty but for some flower vases. After Cremer had gone I opened the drawers. In one of them there was a photograph album. Throughout my childhood and up to my father's death my mother liked taking photographs, and most of these pictures showed my father and me, a serious-looking man of upright bearing and a child growing until it was taller than he was. There was nothing about them to suggest that one would kill himself and the other spend his whole life in a swimming bath. Beneath the photographs were dates, and the dates were crossed out. Only the dates under photos of my mother were still legible.

I took the album into the kitchen and laid it across the top of the rubbish bin, as it was too big to go in. Then I went back into the living room to switch off the light, and caught sight of the picture of my father as a young man in uniform, which had always stood on the television. I pulled the door to behind me. The door to the bedroom was already shut; my mother was still lying there. They would come for her tomorrow, the undertaker's man had told Cremer and me. Until they did, I stayed out of that room. My job was to see that no one drowned. The dead are not my concern.

The Public Baths and Swimming Pool has been closed, the bathers have stayed away without as much as a murmur of protest, no one has complained. For weeks the building has been standing empty and entry is prohibited. And yet I can clearly see people sitting up in the gallery, turning to each other and talking quietly, leaning on the rail in front of them and gazing into the empty pool as if intent on the outcome of a race. At the opening of the baths there were swimming competitions and displays of synchronized swimming, but that was almost a hundred years ago. By the side of the pool, too, I sometimes see pallid swimmers hugging themselves as though they were feeling cold or ill. At times I think the dim light is playing tricks on me and they're not really there, but yesterday I saw the old lifeguard, my predecessor, up in the gallery. When I called to him he turned away without answering, and then was gone.

The building has so many different rooms and areas that it takes me a long time to go through them all, and I don't set foot in Frau Karpfe's office. It isn't clear what's going on, just as in the past things took place here that nobody would ever admit to knowing about. I won't put up any longer with people making a fool of me and letting the building fall into decay. Not just the pool itself, that whole part of the building is sinking, and you can see cracks appearing in the walls. A second slab of plaster broke away from the wall this morning. No one is aware of it yet, but soon the empty pool will reach its lowest point, below ground level, and drag the whole street down with it. The notices posted up here are no use any more, their warnings are wrong. One notice says: *Take care when using the pool steps!* But the two step-ladders that are still in place in the pool no longer reach the bottom. The water shouldn't have been let out. Two-thirds of the earth is covered by water, and water is the same everywhere. Do you hear? You can't deceive me. The dead don't belong here. No one drowned while I was the lifeguard here. I had to come back. In all those years I learned to pay attention to what was going on at the edge of my field of vision, and I can see it clearly. A few days ago I saw the old lifeguard in the corridor leading from the entrance to the pool hall. Soon the bathers will come back and ask where the water is.

It's nighttime now, even if it doesn't get dark in here. That's because of the light from the street lamps. In here day and night look the same, you just hear it getting quieter outside, and inside the rustling gets louder, that's the mice, and rats. The rats are only waiting to be left undisturbed. Then they'll gnaw through the electric wiring.

In the mornings the surface of the water used to lie there as motionless as if no one had ever disturbed it. It was lovely to look at, with the brightly gleaming tiles.

Is it nighttime? I wish I were asleep: in your sleep it's easy to imagine that tomorrow will be a day like any other. On my way to the Swimming Baths I'll stop at Cremer's kiosk, "Guten Morgen, Hugo, Good morning," comes Cremer's greeting as he pushes a bag with two rolls to me across the newspapers. He may read me something, or we'll exchange a few words, before I continue on my way to the baths, which are still deserted. The surface of the water is as calm and undisturbed as if the world had not yet been created, then the first voices can be heard, just one or two, quite hesitant, and usually the first person softly calls out a "Good morning!" to me before climbing cautiously down into the water, for in the morning everyone senses that the water is a foreign element, that it washes away the night and all that has happened and preserves it beneath its mirror-smooth surface, as imperceptible as a smell that one could scarcely detect except through long familiarity. The water has a smell, have you noticed that? It's very faint, but it still persists here and doesn't go away.

It's getting late; I'll go down to the basement now, to sleep. Do you hear me? I'm talking loudly enough, after all, it must be possible to understand what I'm saying. I won't turn the light on, although the passage is very narrow and has a low ceiling. But in the basement there are the four globes, and although two of them have gone out, there's still the light of the other two. How quiet it is. Time drags interminably. This morning a second slab of plaster broke away from the wall. Do you hear? If something isn't done soon, the walls will cave in. There's already that notice at the entrance: *Warning! Danger of collapse!* They'll bury everything beneath them. It's getting late.

Chapter two

The clock has stopped. Previously you could hear it ticking when the pool area was empty, and you could tell what time it was.

I never arrived late. I was always the first to get there and the last to leave; I never missed a day, never asked for any holiday and actually refused to take any. In the mornings I used to leave the house and come straight here without stopping on the way: pausing at Cremer's kiosk doesn't count, since we'd known each other for so long that few words were needed between us.

"Guten Morgen, Hugo! Good morning, Hugo!" he would call and immediately pass the bag with my lunchtime rolls to me across the newspapers. Only occasionally would we exchange a few remarks, and even more rarely would he read me something out of a magazine or newspaper. I've never been much of a talker, and up to the time when the pool was emptied, up to my mother's death, he didn't get much more than a "Good morning!" from me, or "It's cold!" or "Regards to your wife".

All the same, he has to be regarded as my closest acquaintance, ever since his daughter Tanja walked to the Swimming Baths with me and soon afterwards insisted on learning to swim. She was seven at the time, but that's almost thirty years ago now.

I never allowed anything to distract me. Even though I never wanted to become a lifeguard, and saw my work at the baths as an unjust punishment for something done not by me but by my father, I never shirked what was my duty.

Now, when I wake up and go into the pool area after lighting the boilers and having a shower, I'm always late. You can only shower down in the basement because up here the water is turned off. I've tried all the taps. The main stopcock for the changing rooms and showers is turned off, and I daren't risk turning it on because the thread is rusty. All the same, the first thing I do each morning is to go to the showers. I always preferred to shower here rather than at home, I left the bathroom to my mother, to her pink curlers and the smell of hair spray and cologne, in fact I did nothing in that flat except sleep there.

Once I'd become a lifeguard, once the books were gone, packed up and thrown away, I had no other reason to spend any time there. I would drink a cup of tea, have a shave and then set out straight away, in a light jacket because it was only a short distance. It was a routine that worked well, however much Cremer laughed at me and the way I hurried to work.

"Anyone would think you couldn't exist without chlorine. It's a wonder you've got any hair left," he would mock, pointing at his own bald pate. Every day I called at his kiosk and bought two rolls for my lunch but never a paper. "You barely know where you live," Cremer declared, and he was right. I never went anywhere but from the flat to the baths and back, the same route year in, year out, but I'd lost all desire for anything else. Always tidy and inconspicuous—it's only lately that my cheeks have fallen in so that my nose juts out sharply and my gray eyes are too large and sunken. Cremer wouldn't recognize me now.

Immediately after getting up I open the boiler doors, poke about with the iron shovel, look for the last remaining embers and empty out the ashes into big buckets—ashes that are grayish-white and dusty and have lost all resemblance to coal. Since I've been staying here overnight instead of going back to the empty flat to sleep, it's been easier to get the fire going in the morning because there are nearly always some embers still glowing beneath the thick layer of ash. I've learned how to fire the boilers, and I've got over my fear that everything might go up in flames while I'm asleep. I can't be criticized for heating the place because it's obvious to anyone with the slightest knowledge of these matters that I mustn't miss a single day and let the fire go out, or everything would freeze up. I'm not leaving the Swimming Baths any more, so that the building can't be willfully destroyed while I'm wandering around the city or spending time in the flat. Of the stone figures, similar to those that one sees with water spurting from their mouths, two have been broken off, two of the water nymphs, with their round-cheeked angelic faces, that support the big-bellied Neptune with a trident. Originally there were eight figures, now there are only six. No one can condone that. It's damage to public property. I know this building inside out. Someone has to prevent it from sustaining further damage.

Yesterday for the first time I actually heard the sound of a slab of plaster and paint detaching itself from the wall, falling and landing on the tiles. Now it's quiet again.

Do you hear? I don't know what the time is. On a normal day no doubt Frau Karpfe would have been lying in wait, eager to catch me coming in late for work. In the past she was never able to accuse me of any wrongdoing or dereliction of duty. Now she could do it easily: unauthorized entry, trespass. He's a nutcase, the caretaker said, so loudly that I was bound to hear, leave him alone, he's mad, he said audibly to Frau Karpfe when she summoned me to ask, as she was required to do, when I wanted to take my holiday.

"Let him stay here, otherwise he'll crack up," he informed the world at large, not looking in my direction.

That's a lie. Somebody needs to be here to prevent everything from falling into ruin, and no one knows the baths as well as I do.

Can you hear me? I'm taking care to stay close to the pillars. If there are microphones concealed here, they are just above the pillars, where the pillar leads up into the arch, above the tiling. One can see clearly where the plaster is a slightly different color. If I stumble, it's only because I have my dirty shoes before my eyes and the rustling and squeaking in my ears, and I'm listening hard because sometimes a trickling sound comes from the walls as though they were disintegrating. There's a faint resonance in the heating pipes, I can't think why. Or perhaps the sound comes from the wooden seats on the stand, which are riddled with woodworm. Deathwatch beetle, it's called. On the tiles underneath the stand there are tiny conical mounds of very fine dust.

Dust has no business in a swimming bath, and it was dust, and the chunk of plaster and bits of mortar, that started off all the trouble.

I would rarely leave the pool area, and if I did, it was only for a very few minutes when there was no one in the water. A bather had left a towel behind and I went down to the basement to find Klaus, who was in charge of such things because the lost property cupboard is in the small room down there. Perhaps the caretaker happened to see me going down the stairs. I was standing with Klaus in front of the aquarium when I heard the shout.

Fearing that something had happened to a bather, I rushed along the passage and up the stairs.

The others had also heard the caretaker's shout and they all rushed to the spot. It was evening and already dark outside; inside the dimmer nightlight was switched on, with the yellowish bulbs reflected in the calm surface of the water. From the office came the shrill sound of the telephone, otherwise all was quiet. Klaus, who had followed me, stood there with his black shoes on. After a moment, before I could say anything—because they had all come running into the pool hall wearing their shoes— they started talking and laughing.

The caretaker had been there, I hadn't. He was the one who'd shouted: I would have said nothing; I'd have tried to conceal the damage, secretly patch up the damaged area.

Then I saw that he had already swept up the loose dirt and got rid of the larger pieces of debris. Only then had he called out.

A big chunk of plaster, a piece of the wall, slabs of paint and mortar had all broken away, leaving a gaping hollow, an empty space where one would have expected to find solid masonry. The walls are not made of stone or brick but of mortar held together by an iron framework. The iron had rusted through. I had never doubted that the walls were of stone, that the building could withstand anything. It was a pathetic sight. The others burst out laughing, starting with the caretaker, who spat, grabbed the poker from Klaus and began to prod at the hole with it. Plaster came trickling out, and in the dim light dust dropped down on to the water like a flock of birds that would not be thwarted of their prey.

I've never talked much, either to the bathers or to my work colleagues. They hardly ever heard me utter so much as a sentence, let alone raise my voice. They had got used to that, and it suited me that they had. But when the caretaker prodded the wall with the poker, and they were all standing in the dirt in their outdoor shoes and treading it all round the pool area, I should have driven them out of there. Did you get that? I will not keep up this silence any longer!

Later the whole crew got together in the office. On any other day they would have gone home already by that time. I could hear their voices and laughter as I swept up, collected the dirt together and gathered up the lumps so that they shouldn't fall into the water. Then I heard a banging of doors and hoped that they were going at last, that they'd forget about me and perhaps in the night I could make good and disguise the damage, so that next day they'd rub their eyes and be forced to conclude that they'd imagined it all. But it was only the caretaker going to the late-opening store; he returned with a bottle of vodka and came into the pool hall to summon me to the office. There the others were standing around Frau Karpfe's desk, smoking and drawing lots for the different Swimming Baths, which they'd be going to after this one was closed down.

There had always been a number of people who worked here, stayed for some years and then disappeared again—cleaners, cubicle attendants for the public baths upstairs, there was also a technician, and a doctor who came once a week. Only two of them had been there almost as long as I had, the caretaker and the manageress. Everyone called the manageress 'the boss' instead of using her name, although a sign on her door read 'Frau Karpfe'. She mostly stayed in her room, she didn't like leaving her office, preferring to watch the entrance through a mirror; there she would sit, large and heavy, on her office chair, invariably in a flowered short-sleeved dress, demanding reports every single day. On rare occasions she would unexpectedly leave her office, moving swiftly and silently on her spindly high heels and suddenly raising her voice, always finding fault; everyone but the caretaker quailed at the sight of her, her fat arms, her short-cropped hair. She would find errors, inadequacies, signs of carelessness; they all cowered at the sound of her voice. She insisted on being told everything, wanted to know about the private life of every member of the staff; she herself lived alone, and Klaus maintained that she was the caretaker's mistress. She hated the water, kept well away from the pool, never swam, sat in the office smoking, watched in the mirror to see who came and went, had eyes everywhere, and would summon the others to her to ask them things, but not me, since in all those years there was never anything to be learnt from me.

Even now she might suddenly emerge from her office or the caretaker's room. She was always on the lookout, hoping to catch me out doing something wrong, and I shrunk from the thought of her grabbing hold of me with arms that protruded massively from her flowered dress and threatening to report me to the authorities. But she could never manage to pin anything on me.

"Here he is!" they shouted, grinning, and "Warning to non-swimmers!" bellowed the caretaker, prodding Klaus in the ribs to make him pass the bottle on to me. They were all standing in the office smoking and passing round the vodka, I was sent out to buy a second bottle and went without arguing.

It was Klaus who took me home, he found my key in my pocket and dragged me upstairs to the door of the flat, so he told me the next day when, for the first time ever, I was late getting to work. Over the hole in the wall the caretaker had nailed a piece of plastic sheeting which rustled when you went past, and when I got there that morning I was forced to watch the others pulling at it and tapping and scraping at the walls.

"Shoddily built," sneered the caretaker. "Who knows what that's covering up?" he said, looking at me, and nobody took any notice of the mess, as though overnight the whole building had become a condemned property whose days were numbered.

In the evening they came back again, led by the caretaker, who announced that today the pool would close earlier than usual, and the others followed him, they took me by the arm, laughing knowingly. They had a bottle of vodka ready, and when Frau Karpfe called us I had no choice but to go with them.

I never talked much, and except for the benefit of the bathers I never raised my voice, do you hear? I made myself inconspicuous, the others got used to ignoring the pool and me, I managed to see to it that nobody gave us a thought or checked who was in the pool and for how long, and that I was neither seen nor heard, while the bathers came and went anonymously without being stopped or asked any questions about their movements.

No one had any understanding of the water, of swimming, of this place, or appreciated the ceiling vault, the ornamented pillars or the lintels with the lion heads. Daylight enters through the lofty arch at the top end of the pool—shoddy materials, was all that the caretaker said, with malicious pleasure, looking at me. It meant nothing to him that for years bathers have come here to be in the water, as though swimming to and fro gave them a sense of lightness, bodies stretched out, faces calm, and in among them children with their games, their cries, the same unchanging gestures, year upon year. I watched some of them as they grew older and finally stopped coming. Now it's quiet, as quiet as the surface of the water in the mornings, as quiet as if they were all dead, and only the cobwebs are growing.

How to prevent a disaster, that's what I learned. But *this* disaster was not of the expected kind, it went beyond my capabilities, dust has no business to be in a swimming bath, and it was the dust and the chunk of plaster and the bits of mortar that started it all off. Now I walk from one pillar to the next, and where once there was water there's now only dust and the resonance of my own voice. Now I'm waiting for the sound that I didn't hear that first time.

As far as possible I ignored the rustling of the plastic sheeting and the damage to the wall. The caretaker delighted in it, he tapped at the edges of the holes with his hammer to get rid of bits that he said were already loose, and I said nothing. Contrary to his previous habit he came to the pool every day, carrying a hammer, and showed his contempt by kicking at the pillars, and the others came too, examining everything as though for the first time, intent on discovering more signs of decay.

In the evening they met outside the office door and would get shamelessly drunk, as though they were leaving for the various other Swimming Baths the very next day. I myself never expected to find another job. They assembled outside the office where Frau Karpfe sat grimly sorting through papers, fearful of having to clear the office and perhaps also of the irregularities that would now come to light, while the caretaker went in and out, opened the plywood and metal filing cabinets and gave the cleaners papers to throw away.

"We're closing down," he finally announced loudly, and left the baths along with the others. Shortly afterwards Frau Karpfe also locked up the office and called my name, and I had to follow her. The others were already sitting round a table in a pub, Klaus among them; they were drinking beer and were soon tipsy, they raised their glasses to Frau Karpfe, and when they caught sight of me the caretaker stood up and shouted: "Here comes the king of the swimming pool!"

It was November, it was raining, not many bathers came, and by early evening the pool was almost deserted, so that the caretaker decided to close the baths earlier than usual. Frau

Karpfe consented, and Klaus, the boiler man, came up to me and said I must join them. It was November, and since then time has got jumbled, become disordered, so that one hardly knows the sequence of weeks or seasons any more. This disorder must have begun back then, just as the start of everything was that sound which I didn't hear the first time. Only a small number of bathers came, I seem to remember, but I'm not sure, for even if there were no fewer than usual, they didn't see the damage, didn't notice the destruction or were untroubled by it. To them the baths were still the same familiar place, whereas to me they were becoming alien and they, the bathers, were figures from another existence who, against the background of those defective walls which offered no resistance to the caretaker's prodding, were reduced to mere shadows. The plastic sheeting with the hollow space behind it revolted me in the same way as some bathers had done, the cracked skin on old feet, the faces lumpish spheres on the surface which in the mornings disturbed the calm reflections of the daylight and in the evenings the silence of the empty pool hall, the tired light of the bulbs which made the water deeper, three meters, four meters, sixteen hundred meters like the deepest lake, as I had once told Tanja, Cremer's daughter.

"Tell me about the sea," she had demanded, pointing to the water in the pool, but I couldn't tell her anything about the sea. The Swimming Baths are just as good as the sea, I declared, and I was proud of the building. Only now do I realize that for years I have been deluded. For I used to think that the Baths were solidly built, the well-spaced arches and vaulted ceiling, the pillars and the pool, and that the water was safe from harm as long as I was in charge. Now, although it was autumn, almost winter, bats started appearing. When I looked carefully at the glass bricks in the arch at the top end of the pool, searching for a gap through which they might be coming in from outside,

Klaus told me that they were roosting in the boiler room and flying along the passage to the pool area. They hibernate in winter, he told me, and seemed surprised himself; but suddenly they would come fluttering out of their niches as soon as the main light was switched off, squeaking mockingly, hollowing out the gallery and the supporting pillars from the inside— which would end in the lions smashing on the tiles—flying about in front of the paler background of the translucent arch and hanging there as black silhouettes, their thin wings quivering. They still sometimes dart around my head when I'm about to go down into the empty pool, so close that I feel the rush of air; they fly up out of the dusty darkness or hang, with bodies folded, behind the pillars beneath the gallery as though proclaiming that the building is doomed.

"Are you coming with us?" Klaus asked me the following day.

The caretaker announced, "We're closing now! Get a move on," he said, turning to me. "The king of the swimming pool is coming too," he called to the others as he followed me to the entrance hall.

Late that night Klaus again took me home.

"We'll have another drink at your place," he said on the way, and I had to tell him that I lived with my mother, and felt ashamed and tried to shake off his hand from my arm.

"I don't care if I don't find a job," I said to Klaus, "and it's all the same to me where I live, why not at my mother's, after all it's big enough for two, it used to be big enough for three."

My father died long ago, now my mother's dead too, there are still curlers in the bathroom, I found her disgusting, but the place was big enough.

"Nobody in our family ever drank," I told Klaus, who was walking along beside me, laughing at me because I lived with my mother.

"What's the difference," I said to him, "the curlers and brushes are just like the ones you see lying around in the changing rooms, I never wanted to be a lifeguard anyway, all those ugly bodies day after day with their sagging flesh and drooping breasts, and then the men who've just got up from their office chairs or the ones all bent over from humping coal—day in, day out, do you hear?" I told Klaus, "Always the same ugliness, and in bathing caps they have white heads and no faces. Too long anyway," I said to Klaus as we arrived at my front door, "you're lucky to be down in the basement. It's the water," I said, "the water soaks up all the ugliness, you can't get away from the water. The water takes its revenge. Day after day the same bodies, a bit of fabric and skin, the wet hair, the fat legs making such an effort to lift the body out of the water, flabby arms hauling themselves up on the ladders."

"What's that you're muttering?" Klaus asked.

"I've been there too long anyway," I answered. "I don't care if I don't get another job."

"All right, take it easy," said Klaus. "You're coming, aren't you?" he asked again the next evening, the others were standing by the entrance, grinning.

"He's coming along!" one of them called out.

"Just leave him be, he's weird," said another.

"Think you're too good for us, do you?" the caretaker asked in the pub when I didn't immediately want to join them in a drink, "We'll soon see who's the first to get his notice."

One night my mother was waiting for me in the kitchen.

"You're drunk," she said, "your father never drank."

I'd been drinking beer and schnapps like the others; I had to lean on Klaus's shoulder.

"What's that you're muttering?" said Klaus, "They think you're stupid."

"He lives with his mother," the others laughed, "he sees so many girls that he doesn't need one of his own."

A few days went by like that, and in the mornings I didn't wake up of my own accord and had to be woken by my mother.

"What on earth's the matter with you?" Cremer asked. Only a few days, a buzzing in my head, voices.

"You're keeping bad company," my mother said, "that's no job for you."

She had always hated my job, but I never wanted to be a lifeguard, I didn't choose it, it was a mistake from the start, and now I've felt driven to come back here as though it's the only possible place for me. Sometimes I see my mother now with her unsteady walk; she never wanted to have anything to do with my job in all the years after my father died, after he hanged himself in the living room like a stranger and I couldn't recognize his face when I cut him down.

Between then and now countless faces and bodies have passed before me, all bathers; in the mornings they arrived one after another, still half asleep, undressing themselves like children, in the afternoons there'd be different ones, sticking their elbows out as if to make sure of having enough room, and late in the evening there were others again, wanting to make up for the day they'd had, and they simply flitted past me, all of them, except that sometimes I would happen to see the last ones again in the street, holding a bag or a plastic carrier, gray figures suddenly showing up in the light of a street lamp before finally vanishing into a doorway or a tram.

I would be the first there in the mornings and the last to leave at night, I took great care that there should be no grounds for complaint, so that neither the caretaker or Frau Karpfe should have any excuse to come into the pool area. I kept my distance from my work colleagues, and only bumped into my mother on the rare occasions when she got up unusually early or went to bed late. I never sought anybody's company, and never talked much: I can't be accused of that. But now there's complete silence here if I don't speak. I miss the water, the bathers have gone, there's not even a boiler man now.

There was never any cause for complaint, no one came to harm through any failure on my part. Only once—during those few days, in fact—we had to make an emergency call to the doctor, but the baths were not to blame, for it was in the changing room that the woman collapsed, with a little shriek, and because she was vomiting it seemed likely that she had simply begun to feel sick. Then I saw that she had brought up blood and that her head was lying in a pool of red. The others came hurrying up too.

"I knew it at once, the other day," the caretaker said that evening, "the stuff in the walls is poisoning us, and anyone who spends too much time in there will be driven crazy." But the doctor had informed us that the woman had a serious illness, and the baths stayed closed until they had been thoroughly cleansed.

"These are stains," my mother said, "bloodstains." She was holding up the toweling bathrobe that I had taken home for washing the night before.

"That's no job for you," she repeated, and I saw how weak she was, still as angry as on my first day at the Swimming Baths, when she left the house without a word, without saying goodbye to me and felt ashamed because the people she knew expected me to learn a profession, to become a passable human being at any rate, but then whispered amongst themselves:

"What else could you expect of a fascist's son?"

I never wanted to be a lifeguard, I went swimming because father attached importance to physical fitness, until he hanged himself and I was told I couldn't go to university because the Commission had rejected me.

"You presumably know why," they said to me, "be grateful if you're allowed to take up an apprenticeship. Is there anything at all you're any good at," I was asked, "coming from a family like that?"

"I can swim," I must have replied, for swimming was the least of all evils, although I never enjoyed it, but in the water I was left in peace, I could just get into the water and swim. From the first moment I hated my work as a lifeguard, but someone has to be there to see that nobody drowns, I said to my mother, but she shouted at me that I'd have done better to see that my father didn't hang himself.

At first I was assistant to the old lifeguard and had to stay for as long as he wanted, then I was the lifeguard myself, and the only one, at that, and if she didn't want to see me she didn't even need to leave the house, because I went out first thing in the morning and didn't get back until late. In the last few years she began to wait for my return; she hoped that everything would change and wanted to talk to me as soon as I came in through the door, but I still didn't talk any more than before.

Every day I would see countless people in bathrobes or naked, ugly bodies in swimming costumes or trunks, and in the mornings I often came across one of my mother's pink hair curlers and was afraid I would see her coming towards me in a bathrobe or naked, so I avoided using the bathroom and just put the coffee on for her and left. She had bad legs and sometimes wanted to show me her knees or some swelling, she would sit down on a kitchen chair and lift up her nightdress, I didn't know where to look and offered to call the doctor, but she wanted help from me, she said, I had never helped her, she couldn't rely on me.

If anyone claims that I've been a drinker, that was only true for a few days, and anyone who says I got into bad company can't blame me for it, because it was the employees of the Municipal Baths, my colleagues, and they were the ones who insisted I should go along with them. I was too old to find another job, they told me, laughing.

It was the first time that I failed to wake up by myself, and my mother knocked at my bedroom door.

"You've been drinking," she said, and came into my room. She looked around it, just as she had done that time when she told me to pack up the books, and now there were no books there, only my old globe standing on the table. I never went into the living room, my father had hanged himself there, and after that there was his photograph on top of the television, in front of this stood a coffee table and two armchairs and a floral-patterned sofa, and in the evenings my mother sat on the sofa in her bathrobe, waiting for me to come and join her. In the last few years she hardly left the house at all, and if she went to the hairdresser's in the afternoon she would leave a note for me on the kitchen table even though I wasn't there to know that she'd gone out, and I never noticed that there was any change in her appearance.

I have spent my childhood and all the succeeding years in that same flat, and nothing has changed, one day the years stopped being distinguishable from one another. Of course one can knock a building down, or a wall, or one can wait for another chunk to fall down, for the walls themselves to collapse, the gallery, the pillars and the grimacing lion heads. If you, you out there listening, are getting impatient and want to demolish the building, you can do so. Anything can be demolished, even a building that's falling down of its own accord. Only my mother's flat will always stay as it was.

"It's been too long anyway," I said to Klaus; I was drunk and stumbled on the uneven pavements, Klaus swore and grabbed me by the arm, it was raining and my shoes were soaked, Klaus tripped, he was drunk too, I took hold of his shoulder as if he were a bather, although he has never swum but stayed sitting in the basement surrounded by the boilers and his two aquariums. The fish swim, he told me, that's good enough.

"Have you seen the faces of the boss and the caretaker?" Klaus asked.

"Who knows what they've been up to all these years . . . the walls!" Klaus said. "Poisoned, have you heard what the caretaker's saying? About what might be in the walls, and that perhaps we'll all be ill and spew up our blood like that woman," and behind your back he said that maybe all those years by the pool had addled your brain. "They're informers," Klaus added. "Who knows what they've got hidden in the Baths. Haven't they been trying to get you to talk?" But I didn't answer.

I never asked people their names, and there is not one name that I remember, do you hear? Had so-and-so been here, they wanted to know, did he talk to so-and-so? I knew the faces and bodies, I knew exactly how a particular bather swam and how long he would go on swimming, and I can recall exactly a particular movement or a shoulder or a pair of feet, but I never wanted to know names. The bathers have a right to swim and to leave again anonymously; anything else about them is none of my business. People's pasts have unpredictable outcomes, whether those pasts are real or false. Because of my father's past I wasn't allowed to study, and his past was the reason for my being declared guilty. It's a matter of establishing the facts, they told me, and with your family background you should understand that. But I had no idea what my father had done, and they didn't tell me. I had never asked him, nor had my mother, and whatever she knew she kept to herself. He hanged himself. His friends were left alone by the authorities; they came to visit my mother and assured her that he had been unjustly treated, he had only obeyed orders, no one could doubt that he meant well. He was a good man, his friends told my mother, and they continued to visit her for some months after his death, but eventually stopped.

You never know what might come of a past, if you don't know whether it's the right past and no one is much concerned as to whether it is or not, if in the tangled web of intentions one past disappears and a different one is invented. At home it was a taboo subject; he served in the war, my mother would say in reply to my questions, and she would point to the photograph. You can see he's in uniform.

At school they urged me to tell them what he had done, refusing to believe that I didn't know. It was in my own best interests to answer, they told me, threatening that otherwise I wouldn't be allowed to go on to university. I was supposed to use my father's past to buy my own freedom, but I lacked the necessary knowledge, and the fact that I didn't do it seemed to fit in with the general picture. But that picture was obscure, I was being punished for my father's past and was groping in the dark in a game that I couldn't win, for by dying he had put himself beyond reach, prevented me from finding out what he had done. I knew that I bore no guilt, but that this wouldn't help me: I bore his past, though I didn't know what it consisted of, and there was nothing that could acquit me. My mother forbade me to talk to anyone about Father, but that was superfluous, since I knew nothing and didn't dare invent a story to make them stop questioning me.

I took my school-leaving exams, and that was the end of being questioned at school, but at the Swimming Baths it started up again: Did I know the bathers, they asked me, had I heard what they said to each other?

Are you listening to me? I never wanted to tell anybody anything, and there is as little to report about me as about my father. If nothing happens there is no past. No one has drowned, and no one can force me to have a history and a past.

The Public Baths and Swimming Pool is an old building, people used to come here to have a bath or to swim, the walls of the Baths are strong enough, I thought, they can hide what has or hasn't happened here, the days go by uneventfully, turning into years empty of incident, faces and bodies plunge under the surface, re-emerge and leave, anonymous figures, mere movements in the water, which always stays the same, and the building too, I thought, would never change, and I'd be able to stay here to the end.

But they weren't walls in the true sense. I saw where the wall had burst open, the rusty iron struts, and I heard the rustling of the plastic sheeting, then went with the others to the pub. Klaus took me home, and suddenly I saw my feet and beneath them the pavement, the large, irregular paving slabs with great gaps between them, didn't know the way, leaned on Klaus, saw with my own eyes that this was my life, those few yards between the baths and the flat, and I understood that they were going to send me packing.

I have seen the way others silently deteriorate, the way they sit silently in the streets and down in the underground. The first thing you notice is their old clothes, hanging off their bodies as though the body had already faded to nothing, until it ends up as a lifeless heap on the pavement, body and clothes no longer distinguishable, and in no time the streets are clean and tidy again. They leave no traces and no imprint, like a swimmer leaving the water, and nobody asks what might have been done, since it's as if nothing out of the ordinary has happened. Nobody says a word. In the Baths, the days followed one upon another, each one the same, as though nothing had happened, no one seemed to notice what had happened. Where there is such a complete consensus, nothing *has* happened, and after three days the baths had never been any different, had always been a crumbling ruin, a ridiculous edifice with flower stems clambering up the pillars to the gallery, and antiquated equipment.

"A filthy hole where they leave us to rot," the caretaker said venomously, grinning contemptuously at the handful of people who were still coming, "attracting flea-ridden types with no bath of their own. Send him upstairs to mind the bathtubs," the caretaker suggested to Frau Karpfe, meaning me, "he probably hasn't got a bathroom at home either."

On four successive evenings they took me with them when they went out, on the fifth day the caretaker gave me the key to the side door, issuing it to me in Frau Karpfe's name and instructing me to keep the pool open until nine o'clock, although he himself closed the main entrance at eight and after that no more bathers could come because the door was locked; the others had gathered in the entrance hall and they left the baths together, Klaus went with them, passing me by without a look or a word, and I was standing just inside the main entrance when the caretaker pulled the great door shut and turned the key.

I wake at frequent intervals and sit up, and I'm reluctant to leave this spot, as though if I did I'd be unable ever to sleep again, not just on this night but on all nights, though I can barely distinguish one from another anyway.

Perhaps it's not my heart that I hear beating so slowly,

but some other knocking sound that still persists in the walls, like the smell of coal in the basement and the faint odor of chlorine, who knows what happens to sounds, to the voices of the people who were once here?

It's over, I think to myself, and I feel like getting up, going outside, circling the whole building as if I had a duty to protect it from the night and the cold.

I imagined that I was protecting people by watching to ensure that they didn't drown. But you keep your eye on one mode of death and take it off all the rest, and just as water evaporates imperceptibly, so, unperceived, a disaster creeps up on you. When the slab of plaster broke out of the wall I wasn't in the pool area.

It's over, I think to myself when I wake up every couple of hours, sit on the edge of the folding bed, and wait for sleep to come.

I have always known that there is such a thing as betrayal, do you hear? If Cremer knew where I am I couldn't be sure that he wouldn't give me away. I never wanted to know anything, for I too would have betrayed what I knew, just as someone betrayed the old lifeguard, and soon afterwards he was falsely accused of having let a child drown, and he turned into an enemy of the state who suddenly disappeared, for good. I took his place, I was the lifeguard, as though it had always been that way, as though he and I were the same person, and since then I have been living his life or he mine. Sometimes it seems to me that ever since I started working here I myself have disappeared. Lying in my room at night I used to gaze at my old globe and imagine that I was somewhere else, as I recited the names of the countries and contemplated the vast blue areas on the globe. Can you hear me? It's so late. One can no longer feel time passing, the water isn't there, the light isn't there whether it's day or night, the clock has stopped, and only the fish are still swimming slowly up and down.

If I leave the Swimming Baths now I'm not sure that I'll find them again. One afternoon a few weeks ago I left the flat, the flat where my father hanged himself in the living room, I left the flat as I did every day, even though I had no job to go to any more and could have stayed at home, and walked aimlessly around the city while my mother was dying, and now I can't go back there any more. The flat is sealed up. *Jumping in from the sides is strictly prohibited! Face towards the steps!* Can you hear me? If you take one more step you're lost. Where the pool was there's an abyss.

It's first light. Early morning, first light in the pool hall, which is still empty. Sometimes I go on lying there in the basement with my eyes closed, waiting to see it before me.

Even if you can hear me, you won't see it any more, because the water isn't there. It was the effect of the light and water together, especially in the winter, even more in winter than in summer, the pale light, looking all the colder for having come in through the windows and the glass bricks, one can see that this light has no warmth, and even the sun shining through the clouds has no warmth. The early morning light doesn't belong to us, it shows white, dead bodies, it's not a light for people, and it has nothing to do with the world, as though each morning were a repetition of the moment before the Creation. Each morning I was amazed at how smooth the water was, it seemed impossible that only the previous evening, just a few hours earlier, there had been people here, and I wondered at the deserted changing rooms, where not one item of clothing, not one swimming costume recalled the bathers' presence, and I loved this moment, when people and their past lives were of no importance, vanished like splashes of water or rings on the surface which disappear without trace, as if once the water is restored to stillness nothing can come near it.

In the mornings, before the bathers came, the water and the pool area were mine alone; I saw how overnight, from each day to the next, everything stayed unchanged, and even if the city had been carted off overnight the surface of the water would have been unaffected, or so I thought. Through the limpid water one could see right down to the bottom, it's more transparent than glass, and only someone very familiar with it can tell from the odor that it stores up everything, because tiny particles detach themselves from each body, combine with the water and cling to the tiles. Everything comes to light in the end, and after the old lifeguard, whose assistant I was, had fled, I came to realize that he was fleeing from what he had seen, and I took his place. His life or mine, it seemed to make no difference whether he or I was here, the lifeguard was just a lifeguard.

I hadn't given him a thought for a long time. He had let a child drown, or so the rumors ran at first, then soon afterwards they said that he was a criminal like my father; he kept watch over people in his previous job, too, but that was somewhere else, one person said, looking at me, and now I was the lifeguard. For years I hadn't given him a thought, until Klaus turned up one morning in the pool area, which was still dark, and for a moment I thought that the old lifeguard had come back.

"I'm the new boiler man," Klaus said, joining me at the edge of the pool and following my gaze with his eyes.

Before, I had never spoken to the boiler men. They entered the basement from the yard and never came up into the pool area, although there is a passage to it from the basement.

When Klaus suddenly appeared out of the dark, I was startled, as I hadn't heard him coming, and he was embarrassed because he hadn't expected to find anyone there before the baths opened. But every morning I would stand at the side of the pool without switching on the main lighting, surreptitiously, because if the caretaker noticed I was there he took a delight in shouting loudly and turning on all the lights. He would laugh suggestively:

"I bet you sneak about in the women's cubicles and sniff at the shower heads. He's never touched a woman in his life!" he would assert loudly if one of the cleaning women or Frau Karpfe happened to be nearby, "It makes him blush to think that they take their clothes off for other things besides swimming, just look what an innocent expression he's putting on!"

When Klaus suddenly appeared in the dark one morning I was startled and thought it was the old lifeguard, because I'd never seen Klaus before.

"I didn't know anybody was already here," he stammered, "I'm the new boiler man," he said, and as I didn't move he came and stood beside me.

No one who has ever come to work at the Public Baths has treated me with anything but suspicion. It was always Frau Karpfe and the caretaker who showed new appointees the ropes and introduced them to the others, and what they said about me I don't know and it didn't matter, I didn't mix with the others and never wanted to. I was quite content to spend all my time in here; I had no reason to look for company. I didn't want to meet up with the others at weekends because at weekends I was here, and for me there were all the places or countries on the globe that had always stood in my room. Every evening I saw how most of the earth's surface is covered with water, and water is the same everywhere. In the Swimming Baths I was practically everywhere, wherever there's water.

I haven't had to forgo anything, I haven't lacked for any-thing, and in the end one has forgotten one's own life—are you listening to me, out there? Whatever might be said about my life would be empty, like someone tracing the shape of his face with his fingers and still not knowing what it looks like. You forget your own life, not that there's much to forget: it would all fit on to one of the warning notices that just have room for one sentence. A single sentence can preserve you—from a disaster; one sentence may be enough to save a human life:

Face towards the steps!

On winter mornings the light is white and cold, even the water is without color, and Klaus's face too was pale on that morning, as pale and immobile as a death mask.

"I'm the boiler man," he repeated, looking at me with a startled expression. It was such a cold winter that the boiler man had to keep on stoking the boilers, yet in place of two boiler men who had been dismissed, as Klaus told me, he alone had been taken on, he was doing the work of two men, he came and went at the same times as I did and took no breaks, so that all the time that I was up by the pool I knew that Klaus was working down below in the boiler room, trudging to and fro between the mountains of coal in the yard and the boilers, laboring with shovel and barrow to the point of exhaustion. In the evenings he sometimes came up after the pool was closed and would sit on the bench that was right by the stairs, because even when he had showered and changed he was still gray and dirty, and it was only on the days when a relief stoker took over from him that he got home before his children were asleep.

"I get two weekends off a month," he told me.

He worked like that for a year. It was winter when he started and December when the Public Baths were finally closed. Almost every evening before going home he would come up to the pool for a moment to see me.

It was in late November that I lost my job.

Nobody had warned me.

There are papers that you have to sign. By signing I confirmed that I agreed to take early retirement. I only realized afterwards what it was that I'd signed, because at the time I couldn't believe that the Public Baths and Swimming Pool would be closed down, I was sure that it was going to be renovated. Klaus didn't warn me. Afterwards I realized that he had known the truth all along and was in cahoots with the others.

Five days after the first slab of plaster had broken away from the wall, Frau Karpfe called me into the office and made me sign a piece of paper. In connection with the renovation of the baths, she claimed, there's no need to read it, just sign, and then they would order chlorine and flocculent in two days' time. That evening the caretaker told me to stay on the premises until nine o'clock and gave me the key to the side door, forgetting that I could leave the building through the basement, as I normally did. The others had gathered on the steps outside the main entrance, I was standing in the entrance hall, and Klaus passed me without a word, without even looking at me. Behind him the caretaker pulled the door shut. Now I know that it was all the same to them how long I stayed or when I left. They didn't want to take me with them any more, that was all.

I didn't know that soon I would have to let the water out. Those were the last days, the last nights when the pool was full of water, but I still believed that they were having the baths renovated. For the first time it gave me an eerie feeling to be left on my own in that great building.

Even now I sometimes find it eerie, and hear footsteps and whisperings. The rows of seats are still there up in the gallery, and the wooden benches on the stand, everything is still in place for the spectators, and sometimes I see people walking to and fro, sitting down, gazing down at the pool.

"Have you been here long?" Klaus asked me. "You don't have anything to do," he said. "Do you look at the women, or what do you do all day? They say you didn't want anyone to share the work with you."

"Count yourself lucky that you aren't in the basement," he said. "No one ever comes down there. No one to talk to the whole day long."

"Do you think they pee in the water?" he asked. "My wife says I stink of coal even after I've had a really good wash."

"I can cook food on the safety valves down there," Klaus said. "You can have some with me if you like. Do you never have a swim?" he asked. "Can you actually swim? Is it true that a young child drowned while you were on duty?"

"I've got two fish tanks," he said. "Do you want to see them?"

"Frau Karpfe and the caretaker are informers," he said. "What I'd really like would be to keep carp and slaughter them," he grinned, lingering on her name, Carp. "Would you like some?"

It's a year since he came, one morning there he was standing beside me, I had no reason to distrust him, and when we were all called to Frau Karpfe's office he positioned himself next to me.

I haven't been into the office since I've been back. They're all in there, crowded together, the caretaker, Klaus, the two men and two women from the bath cubicles, the cleaners, of whom I only knew Christa who cleaned the pool area, they've got a bottle of vodka that they're taking it in turns to drink from, and I bought the second bottle.

On the day when the first chunk of plaster had broken out of the wall they all gathered in the office.

"You'd better keep your lifebelts with you all the time, who knows," one of them said to me, "if you don't, those snotty youngsters might drown in the dust."

"That's nonsense," shouted another, "but when they come

looking for us among the rubble the first thing they'll spot will be the red and white lifebelts!"

"In a pit disaster," said a third, "you're trapped for days on end until you suffocate."

"*He* knows the building best," one of them said, pointing at me, "he must show us the escape routes."

"Is it true," Christa asked, "that you were born in the Swimming Baths?" and they all laughed.

I can see them before me, just as I see the wall, the gallery, the window arches and the ornamental details, do you hear? And the next day they went to a pub, we all went to a pub together.

"Here comes the king of the swimming pool!" the caretaker proclaimed loudly, the others laughed, and Klaus, the boiler man, brought me home.

They walk away down the street, and for a while you can still hear them calling out to each other, and their footsteps, the clatter of the women's shoes on the pavement, it's easy to pick out the tapping of Christa's high heels; the women pretend to stumble and hang on to the shoulder of the nearest man, and when a pedestrian approaches they crowd him off the pavement, and if he dares to protest they grab hold of him and toss him between the parked cars so that he's lucky if stays on his feet, clinging to the rain-spattered bodywork of the cars, another push and he's lying flat in the gutter.

They deliberately set the woman on me, it was Christa, in the pub she was suddenly sitting on my lap and trying to kiss me, they roared with laughter, Christa's hand trying to fondle my neck, sliding down my chest, their howls and shrieks, I tried to shake her off, their gaping faces all round, I can't remember how many of them there were, a monk, one of them jeered, shit! The caretaker bellowed across to the other tables, "We've got a eunuch here!" "Rubbish," another one interrupted, "he's a queer!" and Christa giggled into my face, her breath, beer breath.

"A tot of brandy for our scholar here!" shouted the caretaker, "Look how pale he is!"

It was a set-up, do you hear? They wanted to see me drunk, lying dead drunk in the gutter, they were just waiting, and they'd been waiting for years to see me make a fool of myself. Even now they won't leave me in peace, they go to my flat at night, they'd like to report me to the police as though everything were my fault. It's just as well that my mother can't open the door to them and is dead. No one knows where I am. They mustn't find me; they'd stop at nothing to harm me.

They made me look a fool, they ridiculed me; when the Swimming Baths began to fall apart with a big slab of plaster and paint coming down, they came hurrying to the spot as though they'd been expecting it, while I still believed the baths were going to be renovated. We all worked here but they didn't care, they abandoned the building without a fight, if something's about to collapse you might as well give it a push!

They were all on the same side, always on the same side, and there was always the water, the sight of it tinted them with a feeling of self-loathing, none of us ever went swimming; the water was there all those years, the same water as when my father was alive, my father was a soldier, he hanged himself, you presumably know why. Back there you'll find the notices, *Jews Not Welcome*, all that was a long time ago, that notice wasn't needed any more, apparently they beat one to death, he sneaked in but they recognized him, the old lifeguard's predecessor recognized him—"There's a Jew there!"—he shouted, or perhaps they drowned him. And I was the lifeguard's assistant later on, or always, it makes no difference how long we've been here because, like the water and the bathers we, too, stay essentially the same.

If he says nothing, then he's got something to hide, said the caretaker behind me, suddenly turning on the ceiling light so that Frau Karpfe's silhouette disappeared for a moment and I swayed on my feet.

"He's drunk," her voice cried out shrilly, "that's what it is." I thought of the swimmers left unattended in the pool area. The caretaker switched off the light and laughed, you can't keep anything from us.

I haven't done anything wrong, do you hear? The Baths are closed now, nobody's going to drown, the pool is empty, and my eyes see nothing and have seen nothing in all these days while I've been walking around the pool. I've been racking my brains as though now I must discover what the crime was, as though I were shut in here for that purpose, because the main entrance will never be opened again, I don't have the key, and even if I had it nobody would come now that there's no water.

A wave of the hand, an order was enough to banish me. No one rebelled, everyone obediently did what was expected, just as I have done all my life, and they kept quiet. I never said much and at most raised my voice to read aloud the words on the notices, I went out with the others when Frau Karpfe demanded it, stayed behind when they wanted me to, and when my mother told me to throw out the old globe I didn't argue.

My room was only the place where I slept, I would come home late, tired and ready for sleep, and in the morning I would just get up again and leave. There's a bed, a small table, a chair, a window, and on the bookcase where my books used to be there was only the globe. When I went to bed but didn't get to sleep straight away I would look at the bluish light, at the continents and the countries, the ocean, those big blue areas. There are places on it that no one has ever seen and that are untouched by anyone because they are only water, which belongs to nobody, and even a traveler who has visited all the countries knows no more about the water than I do, because I saw it each and every morning, that motionless surface, untouched as it had always been. Do you hear? I realize now that nobody knows more about it than I do, and I am not going to let myself be chased away like a dog.

They left without a backward glance. The caretaker locked the main door and no one said a word. The others didn't know that I often left the building through the basement after everyone else had gone, or that the caretaker had given me the key to the side entrance, they thought that I'd be locked in all night. The next day Klaus sneaked upstairs to ask if I'd slept here. Of all the people who ever worked here he was the only one who had been friendly, and when my mother decided it was time to throw out the old globe I took it and carried it through the back yard of the baths, past the coal and into the boiler room and gave it to Klaus to look after. I knew that he kept fish, and where someone keeps fish why shouldn't there also be a globe, even if the borders and names on it aren't right any more.

Borders change, and without walking a step, without getting up and going anywhere, you wake up and find yourself in a different country, I understood that all right, if you don't keep up you get left behind. Everything finally sorted itself out, you don't have to worry, and in the end nothing has ever happened. There's only one border. I understand that now: it's water, water and decay. In the water the death-fish are waiting, if you don't believe me you can go down and look in the basement, they're swimming up and down in the aquarium, they should have been dead, should have starved to death long ago, but time has stopped; like the water, it leaves no traces behind, only invisible ones, hidden from sight, and everything is still there, everything is preserved in the smell of the water which lingers on the tiles, on the walls, and in every part of the building.

Recently, I found three globes in a shop that was closing down; they were being thrown away, as though the earth weren't needed any more now that its borders had shifted, as though it were possible to forget how the world was for some years, just as my father tried to forget the people who died and what he had done, and I tried to forget everything that I was not and now never would be. A whole life can go awry, and an event that is quickly forgotten can result in a whole life being destroyed. People submit to it and wait for the demolition, for decay and the wrecker's ball as though this were a destiny imposed on us. They duck their heads and crawl out of the wind, crawl to where it's dry, they think only of protecting themselves, and read the wrong warning notices out loud, as I have done. But now I don't care. Anyway, in a shop that was closing down I found three globes, and now they're in the basement alongside my old globe and the aquarium. I won't let anyone chase me away.

The tiles are loose. I can hear that plainly whenever I cautiously descend the steps into the pool. They clink like broken crockery or small stones, treading gently doesn't help, you can still hear it, a disturbing sound, it's like broken crockery, like smashed windows, no one would take any notice; one of the stone figures on the front of the building has been knocked off, the whole building can be damaged with impunity, and if the door gets kicked in then anyone can come in.

So far nothing has happened. But they're all here—the caretaker, Frau Karpfe, the cleaners, the women bath attendants and Klaus—they stand outside the building with angry faces, and sometimes I can hear them talking loudly on the steps, in the entrance hall, in the office. They sniff around like dogs, sniff and nose around, picking up the scent of every wound, every weakness. Although I never wanted to go to a pub with them I went along; although I was conscious of their mockery I went with them, sat at the same table and got drunk with them. I had never drunk before, Klaus had to see me home, it was four nights in a row, I was never normally out so late, I'd never seen the streets at that time of night, the lights inside the big windows, the smoke, the people, so many people, and lots of pubs that we passed. We were a group of eight or more. The others had already been drinking beforehand.

"You will come with us, won't you," Klaus said, and the caretaker and Frau Karpfe shouted for me to come. For four days in a row they took me along with them, and in the mornings when I arrived they grinned as though they knew that I hadn't woken up of my own accord. In the morning I was just thinking about the notices, and there was my mother standing in the doorway, coming to wake me up. But I arrived just before the first bathers.

Bathers were still coming.

An elderly man bade me a stern good morning before swimming without stopping for half an hour, climbing out of the water and departing with a curt goodbye.

A young man swam up and down, taking great care to keep close to the side rail as if he feared he might go under at any moment.

The glass swing doors were pushed violently open and three children raced towards the pool as though they were about to jump in fully dressed.

A woman showed her friend her flabby thighs and gave an irritable laugh.

A skinny child with a sly face, squatting on the steps of the non-swimmers' pool, was dabbing saliva off the corners of his mouth with his finger and then dipping it into the water.

Some young people, swimming calmly and confidently, called out something to me in a friendly way and swam on.

An old woman read out, in a piercing, angry voice, the words on a notice: *Jumping in from the sides is strictly prohibited!*

Bathers were still coming, and they seemed not to notice the damaged spot. They were unconcerned about it, swam, dried themselves, and they left, while I stayed there.

Every day I used to read the notices, the warnings and instructions. The rules in a swimming bath are not hard to understand, and because they're easy to obey they are easy to enforce, and there's no room for any confusion.

Ultimately it's the water that determines the rules, nothing else, it makes no difference who the lifeguard is, and it's because a human being is capable of drowning that the lifeguard is there. It's unthinkable that anything about such a place could change, no matter what happens. There must be a place that's always the same, that's not subject to arbitrary decisions or even to time itself, it must be unthinkable that such a place should be built of anything but stone, unthinkable that it should rot and decay like other buildings, houses whose balconies and other projecting parts are knocked off, factories or refineries or gas containers or walls that get blown up.

As long as the water is there nothing will happen, I thought, trying to stay calm, and finally we all gathered in Frau Karpfe's office, we're the people who work here, we all sat in a pub in the evening, they called to me to join them, as though different rules were in force now, because a swimming pool simply can't decay, the water is there, and no one can possibly have such plans, the baths are going to be renovated, I thought, for after all the pool was full of water and it's unthinkable for it not to be.

But on the fifth evening they went off and left me behind on my own, even Klaus walked past me without a word, it was the caretaker who locked the door, and the others didn't know that he had given me the key to the side door. As far as they knew I would be locked in the baths until the next day.

But the pool was still full of water.

On the morning of the sixth day my mother came into my room. I was already awake but still in bed and making no move to get up. I had never been ill and never missed a day; now I wanted to be ill, not to move, not to get up and not to know what there was to get up for, I didn't want to set a foot outside the door or place one foot in front of the other, only to stay in the room. The room stood still as if it had been left behind in some corner that time had overlooked or considered beneath its notice, just as the days push each other along from behind and telescope into each other, I thought, and I gazed at the blue light of the globe which had always stood in my room and steadfastly ignored any shifting of borders. As I had not left the house at the usual time and my mother had woken up before me she came into my room that was illuminated only by the globe and turned the light on, and I saw that she was wearing a flowered dress. I've never been ill and never missed a day, my dismissal notice stresses that point, so on this day too I got up and was at the pool by the proper time. I got up and when I came out of the bathroom my mother had opened the windows wide to let in some fresh air, and she had put the globe by the front door of the flat for me to take down to the dustbin.

"The countries on it have been wrong for a long time, they've got different names now," she said crossly, holding some pairs of swimming trunks, which I found on my bed that evening with new elastic in them. Despite the cold I was sweating as I walked nervously along the icy streets to the back yard of the baths and opened the heavy metal door; I was carrying the globe under my arm, so that Klaus laughed when he saw me, because a lifeguard with a globe under his arm looks funny, he declared, and he was relieved that it was me and not Frau Karpfe, whom he couldn't stand and who, he said, objected to his cooking on the safety valves.

"At Christmas I really will buy some carp," he said mockingly, pointing to the two aquariums in the tool store. In one of them the catfish were swimming in water from the swimming pool, in the other were the small thin fish. When I asked him to look after the globe for me, he went and put it in the tool store.

"If that's what you want," he said, shrugging his shoulders, "but it won't be for long now anyway. Some people are coming from the Department of Public Buildings." He turned away, embarrassed; perhaps he was ashamed of the previous evening and of having passed me without a word. He took the globe and stood it on the table next to the aquariums.

"I'll look after it," he said. But after that he never talked to me any more.

After a few days it was as if nothing had changed, except that the baths closed earlier and I stayed behind on my own. But then Frau Karpfe refused to order the necessary chemicals, the chlorine and flocculent, although everyone must know that the water quality is absolutely crucial. I don't believe in coincidences. Frau Karpfe had promised to forward the order in two days if I signed the paper. I signed it. They knew what they were doing. The water offended them, and they wanted to see it polluted. Frau Karpfe and the caretaker and all the others who worked at the baths were just waiting for it to turn cloudy. They deliberately placed obstacles in my way and failed to order new supplies of chlorine and flocculent so that the water would finally reach an unacceptable level of pollution and then I could justifiably be sent packing. A lifeguard who lets the water get polluted is no better than one who lets a bather drown. Dirt trickled out of the walls, and the caretaker's plastic sheeting added to the damage, since he made it an excuse to fiddle about with a hammer and nails several times a day. It was sheer hypocrisy on his part to claim that he meant it for the best. He invaded the pool area with his outdoor shoes and his tools, and it unsettled the bathers, because if they themselves hadn't noticed any change he drew their attention to the damage and to the generally bad state of the baths. Soon some of the bathers took to making sarcastic comments. Not many, but a number of them turned against the baths, questioning the quality of the water and claiming that their health was being put at risk, no one in the West would be expected to use a pool like that but of course *they* had to put up with just anything, and this would never have happened in the old days. Whenever the caretaker heard them he nodded and urged them to complain, sent them to see Frau Karpfe, and did all he could to stir up feeling against the baths.

"There have been some," he said, meaning me, "who've refused to see reason and selfishly opposed any improvements." And he would wait for them to get dressed and then escort them to Frau Karpfe's office.

Soon after that the building inspectors came, and the authorities responsible for public baths sent their officials to examine the pool and the quality of the water.

At one time the caretaker used to boast about the fact that no one had come from the West to lay down the law and demand redundancies, he wouldn't let anyone tell *him* what to do, he boasted, and thanks to him and Frau Karpfe everything was continuing as normal and nobody was interfering with the People's Baths.

But now they were both waiting and clearly had everything carefully planned, because for days before the officials came Frau Karpfe sat in her office putting some papers in order and destroying others, and the caretaker carried piles of papers past the pool and down into the boiler room as though the pool hall were an office corridor. Perhaps they had been waiting for the moment that best suited their plans. I know only one thing: before the inspection they deliberately did all they could to make the pool hall look run down and so present it in the worst possible light.

At the appointed time, when two men sent by the Public Baths Authorities were due to arrive, Frau Karpfe put on a short jacket on over her flowered dress, bustled into the pool area and then back to the entrance and probably waited for them on the steps outside, with the intention of showing them around the building herself after first taking them into her office. Their voices carried right into the pool area, then there was a long period of silence, and two hours later the officials came into the pool area with the manageress and the caretaker, laughing uproariously about the bathtubs with their curved feet, which they had already seen, and they laughed even more uproariously at the changing rooms and the benches there with cracks which, they said, still had the shit from Göring's behind stuck in them, and Frau Karpfe and the caretaker walked along beside them like servants welcoming their new masters, joining in their laughter. They came in their suits and outdoor shoes, stayed barely a moment.

"Good God!" I heard one of them say, then they went to the steps leading down to the boiler room.

"There's a stink of fish," the other one said, stopping in his tracks, "Get the water tested!" they demanded loudly, ignoring me.

I tried to waylay them as they went out, perhaps they hadn't noticed me, had mistaken me, in my bathrobe, for a bather, but they had no questions to put to the lifeguard, perhaps they didn't know that the water quality is absolutely crucial and that it's the lifeguard's responsibility.

"Complete overhaul or closure," they were already saying as they went round, estimated costs, they walked in their shoes to the very edge of the pool and shook their heads.

"It's not worth it," one of them declared loudly to the caretaker, then they turned towards the exit. I followed them, wanting to explain everything, but they seemed not to see me, they turned their heads momentarily in my direction but didn't look at me, only Frau Karpfe gave me a threatening frown, and the officials went on their way. Perhaps you can tell by the look of someone that he's never been much of a talker, you might think he's dumb, or stupid, and the upshot is that he might just as well not be there.

I ran out of chlorine and flocculent, and fewer and fewer bathers came. I saved the empty containers, as though they would fill up again by themselves, unscrewed the tops and sniffed, but even the chlorine smell grew weaker, the water was already starting to turn cloudy, and I had a suspicion that Klaus was no longer heating the water properly, that he was neglecting the boiler which supplied it. More and more often I found myself alone in the pool hall, it was only in the afternoons that a few old people and mothers with children came, perhaps the others had found a different swimming pool, were going to the City Baths or had given up swimming. I listened for the sound of the main entrance door, suspecting that the caretaker was stopping bathers in the entrance hall and turning them away, just as for a time he had turned away anyone without a bathing cap. Often when I was alone in the pool area I sneaked out to the entrance hall, found no one there and came back, and the surface of the water was quite still, which was not a good sign in the middle of the day.

But a lifeguard must never relax his vigilance, even if all that remains is what has *not* happened, clear water, cloudy water, the fear of what could happen at any time. The surface of the water lies there motionless and untouched, and if you look into the water you see only what lies beneath it, the tiling, turquoise but not evenly colored, which can make you believe you're looking at a lake on which barely perceptible ripples catch the light and make it dance. It's only an illusion. You think that the water retains no traces, but you know that everything breaks down into minute particles that are invisible to the eye so long as you choose to see only a smooth surface offering no hint of anything else.

That is what I saw, day in, day out. The lifeguard is responsible for ensuring that nothing is lost and that the water stays clear. He must anticipate any clouding before it happens. For if you can see the water, what you are seeing is not the water itself but what damages it, and once it succumbs to pollution there is no remedy. Then you've got to drain it off, the old lifeguard explained to me, so as to let the pool dry out, preferably for several days. That means the baths can't operate normally, and sometimes a tile comes loose or you get cracks developing.

"Do you notice the smell?" he asked. "Nothing has been lost. You can still smell what happened here. Can you smell the water? When the pool is emptied out the smell lingers on the tiles and in the joints between them. I've seen the pool empty," he told me, "after the war the pool was empty and it stank. Do you know what went on here? They didn't use the pool for swimming. But they kept people imprisoned here. You'll do well to make sure that the water stays clear. When the water gets polluted you smell all the stuff that the bathers bring in. And it hasn't always just been bathers, I saw it with my own eyes. They locked people up in the basement and then murdered them. The corpses were lying here in the pool. I had to remove them and clean up the pool. Then we let the water back in again and everything was just as it had been before. It wasn't long before the first bathers came again. I recognized them, they're still coming," the old lifeguard told me.

"They think the water washes everything away, but if you know the water you can smell where they've come from and what they're carting around with them. The water stinks to high heaven, even if no one's prepared to admit it," he said, and at first I thought he'd taken leave of his senses.

But I saw the water every day for almost forty years. I know that he was right, and perhaps Frau Karpfe and the caretaker knew it too. They kept clear of the pool area, and they never swam. They wanted to see the whole building demolished. They planned it. Now it's as quiet here as a graveyard. The dead are not my concern. As long as I was here no bather ever drowned. But now that the pool is empty it's impossible to deceive oneself about the smell, and they are all appearing here again and looking around expectantly as if they must surely be remembered here. They turn their heads to right and left, flit by like shadows or stand rigidly at the edge of the pool, paying no heed when I call. The silence is unbearable.

I cut my father down myself, who else was there to do it? I couldn't save him, I didn't want to, but I have not let anybody drown. Here it was usually noisy, lots of children came, they splashed, yelled and quarreled, the grown-ups also talked loudly and shouted to each other across the pool. There were nearly always people here. I thought no dead person would find his way in here. But the dead *are* here, they stand at the edge of the pool and know that they are not welcome. If the building is demolished no one will remember them or what happened here. The old lifeguard had a predecessor; I am the third lifeguard here. The Public Baths are closed and I've been dismissed. The old lifeguard disappeared a long time ago. They came to get him. At first I thought he'd gone mad, but now I realize that he was right. Only a few streets away there's a water tower where they killed people. They've put a plaque there now for everyone to read. The water tower was taken out of service directly after the war. But the People's Baths were soon in use again. For close on a hundred years this building has provided People's Baths and a swimming pool. People have always come here. I have seen acquaintances of my father's here. They are dead now. I never gave any sign that I knew them. I never spoke to anyone. I didn't attend my father's funeral. When my mother came home she screamed at me that I shouldn't forget that if circumstances were different he'd have been given a state funeral. Circumstances had changed. They have changed again. He's an informer, Klaus said about the caretaker, as if he had known him before. That's nothing to do with me.

I was only concerned to see that the rules were obeyed. What the notices say is limited to a very few instructions which no one can misunderstand. Once there were other notices, the caretaker brought them out of Frau Karpfe's office: *Jews not welcome!* He set them up in the entrance hall, grinning. In the evening I removed them. They are still in the little storeroom. No bather has ever been refused entry by me. I didn't know their names and didn't want to know them. The bathers come, they swim, and the lifeguard makes sure that they don't go under. Where they come from is all the same to him.

You can tell from the way they swim: they've been rushing around all day, they've come from home or straight from work, they have an air of satisfaction or not, they draw their arms back in the water as though preparing to punch someone, or their hands reach out for an embrace, they breathe slowly as if they were still hearing an angry voice, cringe, even now, in the water or swim at top speed as if to force the end of the pool to retreat; another face grows old with sadness, you hear scraps of sentences, the window broken, a friend ill for weeks now, hope with each new day, a mother slaps her child's face, a child fights with another, the flat's too cramped, can't find a new one, they climb out of the water, dry themselves, towels tidily hung over their arm or crumpled like a piece of paper, get dressed again and go.

Towards evening I would hear Frau Karpfe's voice when she was about to leave, always a little early, and the caretaker laughing in the entrance hall, before they all set off for home and it quietened down. That left just one of the attendants looking after the individual baths, the boiler man, who was still there, and me. A part-timer was still at the cash till counting the day's takings, letting the last bathers out and nobody else in, the splashing of disturbed water grew less, one of the showers could still be heard running, then muted sounds of movement in the changing rooms, *Guten Abend*—Good night . . . and the last footsteps in the corridor leading to the entrance hall, while the water grew still like some great beast whose coat is ruffled by a tremor as it dozes. Then I turned off the main lights, I'd changed the sandals for trainers, they made no sound, and finally I stood for a while at the edge of the pool, there was no need to keep watch now, and the water lay still. Nothing could happen overnight.

By the time I got home it was half past nine and almost time to go to bed because I'd be up again at six in the morning. I didn't read, there were no books there, and I put out the light, leaving only the globe switched on, lay on the bed and gazed at the illuminated sphere, which shone brightly in the dark room, at the blue-painted areas that represent the sea. Water predominates, it takes up more of the surface than the land, and Cremer read an article to me, which said that there's water even under the desert. It said that the icebergs are melting and the water level rising, and that in the not-too-distant future there'll be huge floods. The blue areas are growing larger and nobody can stop them. In the end there'll be water here in the pool again too. A black line across the floor of the pool separates the swimmers' and non-swimmers' areas. A red line round the edge acts as a warning to anyone not to take a rash step. On the globe, too, you can see exactly where the land ends and the water begins. The other borders are irrelevant. I refuse to let myself be distracted.

The other people working in the baths laughed at me because I would be the first to arrive and the last to leave and never had anything to say for myself. They called me taciturn or uncommunicative or dumb, and would sometimes voice the suspicion that I considered myself above talking to the likes of them, or that I had reasons of my own for keeping quiet, and finally they accepted the caretaker's explanation that I was feeble-minded and only capable of parroting the words on the warning notices. And I was glad that they left me in peace, hardly ever came near the pool and so brought no dirt in, for anything that is on the floor can so easily get into the water and clog up the filters, you have to keep the filters clean, without filters the swimming pool water is a lost cause and no amount of chlorine or flocculent will do any good. You have to judge exactly which chemicals to use and how much, everything depends on using the right product at the right time, especially when the water is in a critical state and more seriously affected by pollution than usual. Anyone who knows the water can tell at once what the quality is like, he needs only to come near the pool or put a hand into the water, just a glance is enough, a touch, a whiff: I didn't need to confirm it by measuring either the chlorine content of the water or its acidity, and when the inspectors came the water was slightly cloudy, it was showing signs of pollution, but the cloudiness was only superficial and could still have been remedied by taking the appropriate measures. But I was prevented, deliberately prevented, from doing my job. Perhaps excellent water quality might have had a favorable influence on the inspectors and inclined them to a less devastating verdict. The caretaker grinned as he told me the verdict: the pool has subsided, the costs of renovation are unacceptably high—the

Baths would have to be closed down. And he went rushing around the building, up to the bath cubicles and down to the boiler room, delivering the glad tidings to one and all, and they gathered around the pool as if for a celebration.

The pool, he repeated triumphantly, pointing to me, the pool has subsided. The water needs to be drained off, he announced, the water's too heavy. The tests have shown that the water's too heavy, he repeated, and he seized hold of Christa's cleaning bucket, raised it above his head and in one sweeping movement emptied the contents, the filthy water and lather, into the pool, and seemed about to throw the bucket in as well. The soapsuds floated greasily on top of the water, a dark-colored current broadened out and gradually dispersed, particles of fluff and other matter swirled about for a while longer before slowly sinking, while the soap bubbles burst, glinting poisonously on the surface, a bit of paper pitched and rolled, then gradually became saturated, a price tag bobbed up to the surface again, the writing on it becoming blurred. I was about to run for my net on the long pole but the caretaker grabbed me by the arm and would not let go.

"Your water is crap!" he mouthed venomously, and spat into the pool as if it were a sewer.

Frau Karpfe and Christa laughed, and Frau Karpfe took her cigarette from her mouth and tossed the stub into the water; it glowed brightly for a moment as it flew through the air, then, meeting the water, went out with a hiss and began to release streaks of brown, while the paper around the filter peeled off like a plaster from a festering wound. The others were standing in a circle around us, I tried to catch Klaus's eye, but the caretaker gestured to him with his free hand and Klaus took a step forward towards the edge, crumpled up a serviette with red ketchup stains on it and, to the accompaniment of laughter from the others, hurled it as far as he could.

They went away without paying any further attention to me. When the caretaker released me I continued to stand there motionless, then I crouched down at the edge of the pool and watched as the water became calm again like a sick patient who, after suffering a spasm, sinks back on to the bed without a struggle. I dipped my hand into the water, the bits of paper were too far out, I couldn't reach them and I didn't get up to fetch the net, the water was cool and lifeless like a corpse, and when I drew my hand out and smelled it my nose was assailed by an acrid smell, cleaning fluids and malice and decomposition, and my hand filled me with revulsion. I did nothing. The water was suddenly alien to me. I felt afraid. In the entrance hall the voices died away as the others gradually left, I heard the door close, then there was silence. I said nothing; the place was as silent as it is now.

Even in the pool I sometimes see people. They walk up and down like prisoners in a yard. Sometimes one of them bends down, runs his finger over the tiles, as I have done myself, then smells his finger, and in the semi-darkness I can make out the movement even if I can't recognize the faces, and when I look directly at them they have vanished. They are shadows, who don't respond when I call them. If there were still water here they would not come. There are dead people among them, and others. Anyone who has been here never gets out again. Even the caretaker was wrong to think that getting rid of the water would be the end of the matter. For I can see him before me, his fat arms hanging down from his shoulders, his red face, his short-paced, noisy walk. And Frau Karpfe too, still half a head taller, morosely smoking cigarette after cigarette, she dyes her short-cropped hair blonde, she's in the gallery standing close up against the wall, holding a file full of documents, and when I try to look in her direction she turns away, not recognizing me. Where else should I go? No one gets out of here.

The sound of my footsteps moving from one pillar to the next is the only thing I hear, unless I say something. The holes in the wall are plainly visible. After I came back here I pulled off the plastic sheeting. It wasn't holding in the dirt, dust continued to trickle from the open gap, and the plastic rustled when you went past. I pulled out the nails too. The paint flaked off where the caretaker hammered the nails in, and there are deep cracks half a yard long. There's no damage to be seen below the gallery, because the wall is tiled up to that level, as it is in the changing rooms. But when you run your hand over the tiles you can feel the unevenness, as though the walls were bulging, as though the internal wall were affected by water damage.

"There's no point in heating the pool area," the caretaker announced the following morning, showing me a notice on a small piece of cardboard:

The swimming pool will remain closed.

"You can let the water out," he said, "or do you want me to do it?"

Although it was chilly I put on my bathing trunks, as I did every day. Then I went into the small room which opens off the first half-landing on the steps down to the boiler room.

I went hesitantly down the steps and had to go back again because I'd left the key in the pocket of my bathrobe. I've always taken care to keep this room locked, because it's where the valves are that control the flow of water into or out of the pool, as well as the filter, and it's also where I store the big containers of chlorine and flocculent. Only the caretaker, the manageress and I have a key, and I used to clean the room myself and do the maintenance on the inlet cock and the outlet valve, keeping them regularly cleaned and oiled so that they wouldn't stick or rust. Once a week I would let some water out and some fresh water in, and only then add chlorine. I cleaned the filter and also the pumps that circulate the heated water back up from the boiler room and into the pool. I kept everything in such good condition that repairs were very seldom necessary, and I didn't need to touch the outlet valve to know that it would move freely, without any resistance.

For a moment I stood outside the room with the key in my hand. Down in the boiler room I could hear Klaus whistling, and from the pool area the caretaker jeeringly called to ask if I needed any help. I unlocked the room, switched on the light, and went over to the outlet valve, which it took only one hand to operate.

When I came out I left the door wide open. There was no reason to lock it now. Back upstairs the caretaker was waiting for me and gave me some big file cards on which I was to list all items in the pool area and the changing rooms that could be transported elsewhere for future use.

"You can keep the life-belt," the caretaker grinned, and went off, leaving me to my own devices.

It takes a long time for a swimming pool to drain completely. The surface of the water stayed motionless as though nothing had happened, and by midday only a very slight change in the water level could be detected by the naked eye, so that the caretaker went into the little control room himself to check whether I had fully opened the valve. Up to midday I tried to convince myself that the water wouldn't flow out, as though it could understand the shamefulness of what was taking place. But I knew very well what I had done and that I had opened the valve to its full extent and that the water was inexorably draining away. You yourself take the decisive step, hoping that it may have no consequences, and when it does have consequences it's too late and you no longer have the strength to do anything. I myself opened the outlet. If I hadn't obeyed the instruction, the caretaker would have done so instead of me.

In the pool hall it got colder, I had to put my bathrobe

on. Not one bather came to protest. At the main entrance, too, the caretaker had put up a cardboard notice, and in the afternoon he placed a big notice in front of the corridor leading to the pool:

No entry! Danger of collapse!

In the evening, the manageress herself collected the completed file cards from me. The caretaker asked angrily why the pool was taking so long to empty.

"Send him upstairs to mind the bathtubs," he said to Frau Karpfe, and she repeated:

"As soon as the pool is empty, you'll go and look after the bathtubs."

Then they left. It was only about six o'clock, and the whole building was strangely quiet.

I sat down on a wooden bench and gazed at the gradually sinking water level. I had switched off the big lights, the pool hall was empty—the scene of a disaster, which people leave without looking back. Sometimes the plastic sheeting rustled in a draught. I noticed the smell coming from the slowly emptying pool. Putrid water now, it's the putrefaction of all the years— all the years since the baths were built.

"Do you understand," the old lifeguard said to me, "it's all still here, nothing washes off that easily. The People's Baths!" he laughed.

"Do you know what happened here once? Look how innocently the water lies there. Some innocence," he laughed. "In the side passage there wasn't room to shoot people. There are still some bathers you can ask if they never heard anything when they passed by the baths while they were closed during the last year or two of the war. There are some who did have access even then. Only those who ended up lying on the bottom of the empty pool can't be asked any more. But if you watch really carefully you may see them sometime. Don't you notice the smell? Nothing washes off that easily, we all still stink of it. Be thankful that chlorine's available again. The particles sink to the bottom and get into the spaces between the tiles. When the pool is empty you'll see what comes crawling out of those cracks."

He disappeared, do you hear? No one protested when the water drained away. I stayed sitting on the wooden bench until late. Next morning I thought for a moment that I'd only dreamed it. It takes a long time for a swimming pool to drain completely. Three days, that's what it takes. On the second day there was still water in the non-swimmers' section. No one came anywhere near the pool. On the third day the water had retreated to the deep end, the tiles in the nearer part glistened with moisture. Then the water level went down to the bottom rungs of the ladders. On the morning of the fourth day the pool was empty. Frau Karpfe called me and sent me up to the individual bath cubicles. I never went into the pool area again until I came back to the baths.

If I hadn't opened the outlet valve someone else would have done it. You can't reproach me for anything. I filled in the file cards and concealed nothing. I included the two life-belts. When the benches and lockers were removed from the changing rooms I wasn't there to see it. The manageress had ordered me not to list the two wooden benches from the pool area. One of them she took for herself, the other is still there.

"Don't forget the water!" the caretaker jeered; that was when the pool was already half empty.

Sometimes it seems to me as if I'd been asleep for weeks. Down below in the boiler room you don't hear a sound; you can't even tell if anyone but you is still alive. Countless people have come and gone here. You want to raise your hand and say something, but there's no one there, and no one turns their head. I don't know if there were informers. Frau Karpfe and the caretaker wanted the pool to be emptied and the Swimming

Baths closed. They can hear every word, Klaus whispered to me, when he still used to come into the pool area. But they aren't even here, I objected one evening, after everyone but the two of us had left. Come off it, said Klaus. They have tapes and it's all recorded.

Do you hear me? If no one keeps the heating going the walls will get damp. The tiles will come loose, fall off the wall and smash on the floor. In the pool the tiles are turquoise and on the walls they're white. The holes in the walls look like wounds, and anyone who thought that the baths were built of stone knows better now. In the night I lie awake and know that the walls consist of iron struts and mortar, and mortar may have anything mixed into it that can be ground to a fine powder— gravel and bone-meal and straw and rags. The People's Baths are built of garbage. It's not my fault if no one comes here any more. I had to let the water out; otherwise the caretaker would have done it. The old lifeguard warned me. Even the individual baths were hardly used any more. They sent me there so that I shouldn't see what they were doing down here. They cleared out the filing cabinets in the office and took some of the papers down to the boiler room. The pool area and the changing rooms have been cleared, there's only one wooden bench left.

"If you don't want to mind the bathtubs you can always leave," the caretaker said threateningly. Where could I have gone?

The people who looked after the bath cubicles never stayed for long. It was always the older ones who did that job, and in recent years only a few old people were still coming to have baths. It's no job for a lifeguard.

Between the cubicles there's a small vestibule. Two attendants used to sit there, a man and a woman, keeping an eye on the clock and chivvying people when their time was up. They ran some water in and cleaned the baths, then filled them with clean water again and stayed on hand in case someone had a fall or called for assistance, because hot water has a debilitating effect on the organism. They wiped the baths to get rid of the worst of the grime, but every lunch-time and evening the cubicles and bathtubs were thoroughly cleaned and disinfected by the cleaning women, and whoever was in charge of the bath cubicles had little more to do than to admit each person in turn and make sure that they left again.

The people who came to take a bath there were old, my mother could have been one of them, but we always had a bathroom of our own and my mother left the house only very rarely. Old bodies smell bad, they smell of loneliness, of illness, you wouldn't want to let them into the pool. They look as if they were sure to die soon. In the pool people don't just die, they might drown, if anything, and that's what the lifeguard is there for.

I had nothing to do. The previous attendants had already been dismissed, and there was no one left to see to the women. Christa had to look after them and grumbled loudly whenever she was letting out dirty bathwater or cleaning a bath, and in the end she told Frau Karpfe that I could perfectly well look after the women too. In the first week there were still five or six people a day, then some of those stopped coming, and in the third week there was only one old woman who always pretended not to see me and became abusive when I knocked after an hour, fearing that she might have died.

I don't remember those days very well. Why should I remember them? The work bears no relation to my proper job: I'm the lifeguard, I don't know anything about bathtubs, I sat in that tiny room with nothing to do, and a dirty sludge hung around for ages in the bottom of the tubs because the plug-holes were blocked. Where I sat it was dark, there's only a meager window high up in the wall, the alarm clock standing on a small table had stopped, I had to guess how time was passing because

I haven't worn a watch since I was a boy. Frau Karpfe was clearing the office, they all knew it was over; I was the only one who wasn't told. I sat up there on the first floor when no one wanted to take baths any more, and throughout the day I didn't speak or hear a single word. Only in the mornings, on my way to work, Cremer would wish me a good morning.

At the entrance to the pool hall stood the notice:

Keep out! Danger of collapse!

Not a sound was to be heard, three weeks passed like this, passed slowly, and I listened anxiously in the hope that workmen would soon be coming to repair the walls around the pool, replace rusted struts, re-examine the pool itself and establish that it hadn't subsided after all, that the inspectors' assessment had been wrong. Frau Karpfe was having to clear her office because it was to be repainted, I thought, and on one occasion I went down there, knocked at her door, found her alone at her desk, on which nothing remained but an ashtray and the telephone, and told her that I had signed it, the request for the chlorine and flocculent, the request for the renovation of the People's Baths. I wanted to ask when the work would begin and where the others were, and I didn't hear the caretaker until suddenly he was right behind me and burst out laughing.

On one occasion I went out into the yard, knocked on the iron door to the boiler room and waited for Klaus to open the door to me; I could hear that someone was there, but no one answered and no one opened the door.

I was in charge of the bath cubicles for three weeks, and during the third week no one came to have a bath. I sat up there all day long, and at the end of the third week Frau Karpfe called to me, waited for me at the bottom of the stairs and handed me a letter from the city authorities. The caretaker was standing next to her, grinning, as I took the letter.

"Do you now realize what it was you signed?" he laughed,

then he went to the door, opened it wide and showed me the notice attached to it with a drawing pin: *As of 30 November, the People's Baths will be closed.*

I was still holding the letter, unopened, when he waved me out through the door. He closed it behind me, and I heard him turn the key.

I didn't need to read the letter to know what it said.

The light in the entrance hall was turned off, the two windows next to the main entrance were in darkness, and it was only further inside, in the office, that a light still burned. I said nothing. The notice gleamed white in the darkness, but I couldn't make out the letters.

It was only seven o'clock. I was never home before nine.

Chapter three

The following day I awoke and got up at my usual time, made myself a cup of tea in the kitchen as I did every morning and put the coffee on for my mother. Then, careful not to make any noise, I went back to my bedroom to fetch my jacket, the light jacket because it's not a long walk. The fact that the walk is short has always made it unnecessary to put on a thick coat, even on very cold days. From a shoebox in the wardrobe I took out a pair of sturdy brown leather shoes that I had never worn. My father was always a firm believer in good shoes, but for a lifeguard, trainers are the appropriate footwear, and so I had one well worn and one newer pair, the first for the walk to work, the other for the baths, though in fact I would wear rubber sandals there during the day. I had never had any occasion to wear the leather shoes and so they lay unused in the shoebox, still wrapped in white tissue paper, just as my mother had given them to me. On this morning I took them out of the box for the first time and put them on. I had woken up at the usual time; as on every other morning I made myself a cup of tea in the kitchen, and I left the flat just as I always did. Going down the stairs I was conscious of my feet not feeling the same as usual and of the clattering sound of the hard, smooth heels.

When I leave the house in the morning I turn left. Soon I've reached the back of Cremer's kiosk, go round it, on either the left or the right-hand side of it and wish him good morning.

He passes a bag with two rolls to me across the newspapers and we exchange a few words. He might tell me, for instance, about what happened the previous day or he might read something to me from a magazine, then I say goodbye to him and carry on to the baths, which will be opening soon because there are people who come very early to have a swim before work. Once I've pulled the door of the flat shut behind me, quietly so as not to wake my mother, and left the building, everything simply follows its normal course.

On this particular morning I had got up at my usual time and I walked in the same direction as I always did, without thinking about it. I went nearly as far as Cremer's kiosk, but when it came into view I stopped, turned round and walked the other way. You might almost think that the course of things is determined by your shoes. It was a fine day, I clearly remember that, it was not raining, not snowing, and cold only because it was winter.

On a street corner a man stood watching me. Just for a moment I thought it could be the caretaker, but then I realized that I didn't know this man and I knew nobody who passed me in the street. I remember walking very fast, as though it were quite normal for me to be walking so briskly from one place to another, as if someone were expecting me. If you walk briskly, distances seem shorter, and if you don't know where you're going you just have to keep walking.

Since for years I had only walked from the flat to the baths and back again I soon had no idea where I was, and I kept walking, because, I told myself, nobody stops without some reason, and so I tried to look as if I knew where I was going.

No one goes out into the street aimlessly, and if you do, you have to try to conceal it, for there are rules, just as there are in a swimming bath, where people have to swim up and down the length of the pool because that's the rule, and anyone swimming across the width of it is out of line and draws attention to himself, because in a swimming pool you swim lengths.

In a pool there are only swimmers and non-swimmers, and the non-swimmers are children and are not allowed to go beyond the non-swimmers' section. I myself would have intervened had someone in the pool started swimming across it instead of lengthways, and I would always keep a close eye on the non-swimmers to prevent them from getting in the way of the others. There are clear distinctions. You don't walk in the streets for no reason at all, and if you go for a walk, you do it on a Sunday or in a park.

You have to breathe regularly when you're walking, just as people do when they're swimming. If they don't they may find themselves choking, swallowing water, and that can have dire consequences if the lifeguard doesn't notice in time.

Regular breathing is important, and anyone who is out of breath must get out of the water. That's why there have to be benches in the pool area, so that anyone out of breath or exhausted can have a rest.

I wasn't used to doing a lot of walking. But when there's no reason to walk, there's no reason to stop either.

Do you hear me? You stop in the street when you don't know where to go. You stand there in the midst of all the people walking past, and looks are directed at you, silent looks, although there's no one keeping watch, for why should anything happen to anybody, everything's simply going on as normal and there's no reason to keep watch, there's nothing to be saved.

All day long, as I walked about, I was expecting to meet Klaus or one of the bathers, and I even looked out for Frau Karpfe and the caretaker; but there were only people I had never seen before.

When you swim you look straight ahead of you and unless you're doing backstroke you keep your eyes on where you're swimming to, on the water or the other swimmers, the wall, the clock, the translucent half-circle of glass bricks, where the light enters evenly through the thick glass. When I stood at the top end of the pool I could see eyes growing calm, faces growing round, heads bobbing like balls on the surface, like floats.

Go right. Turn off to the left there.

No one said anything. I thought I ought to ask someone the way, but people seemed in such a hurry, crossing streets, entering buildings, shops, taking one step after another. I couldn't recognize a single face; turn left at the next junction and you'll be there. But there was no place I could ask for, though I really wanted to ask for the swimming pool, and if someone could have answered me and told me where to find it, then everything would have been as it was before.

The streets soon began to look alike, not even their names were familiar, I went on, didn't know where I was, I felt uneasy and it was cold. In here it's always been warm, there's still a wooden bench here, anyone who wants to rest can do so, because in the water an exhausted person would drown fairly quickly. He wouldn't make it to the pool's step-ladders.

I was afraid I might not find my way back, I didn't recognize the buildings. On that day I kept to the main streets and ended up walking round the sides of a square, which was something I was used to, since I was used to walking round the pool, because if you stand still or sit down you rapidly lose concentration and soon start feeling drowsy. So it's better to keep circling round, and you mustn't be thinking about your steps as you take them, they need to be regular and effortless, because any tripping or stumbling would be a distraction and a danger. A lifeguard is used to being observant, but what happens out in the street or inside the buildings is no concern of his—hardly anyone ever drowns in the street or in the bath at home. A person doesn't drown in his bath unless he wants to, and he can just as easily hang himself, but none of that is the lifeguard's concern; not for that matter, life itself, or, with very few exceptions, death.

Outside the Swimming Baths a lifeguard's alertness is not required, and anyway, it seemed as if all these people knew where they were headed, and I was the one who didn't know which way to go or where to aim for. No one approached me either to seek or to offer help, and the hours dragged by even more slowly than when I had been looking after the bath cubicles. It was there that I had started becoming aware of time. Now the day was never-ending. Under my trousers I was wearing my swimming trunks, because if someone jumps into the water from the side then disaster is not far off.

"You barely know where you are," Cremer had said to me accusingly when the Wall came down, and he asked me if I even knew what country I was living in.

Like many others I thought that on the very next morning I would come to the Baths and find everything changed. Perhaps there were places where everything really had changed. But at the Swimming Baths nothing had changed. Some people stopped coming and others gradually took their place. The individual baths were used less. The swimmers had new swimsuits, even the coloring of their faces and bodies was not the same as before.

"In my job, it makes no difference," I answered Cremer, and after all he himself was still sitting where he had always sat, in his kiosk.

"Anyhow, what would you expect to be different at the Baths?" I continued, knowing the answer myself.

The tiles are still there. The water would take on any color as far as appearance goes, but in fact it remains stubbornly true to itself, and when you drown, if not before, you'll realize that it hasn't changed. Yet I continued to ensure that no one drowned while I was on duty. It was only when plaster started crumbling from the walls that everything changed: a whole building only fit for demolition.

I have never liked swimming, as a child I hated it, but I hated games even more, ball games, the bruises and the shouting. For swimming you have to get undressed, and my father could no longer beat me whenever he felt like it.

There was no way of evading my father's commands, since he would wait for me even when I had already overtaken him in height. He would wait, stick in hand, he knew the commands, and he'd be waiting for me in the hall before I knew what I had done wrong, in that same flat, my mother behind the bedroom door, behind the living room door my father, hanged, with my mother waiting in the hall until I had cut him down, and I thought everything had changed, at last I would do what I wanted. I stopped going swimming, I applied to become a student, only to return soon afterwards to the Swimming Baths, different baths which were to be my last, because now I've been dismissed, not transferred but forced into early retirement.

I walked round and round the sides of a square, but from across the road and above the noise of the traffic no one hears if you call out. I could see the children playing, quite a number of children in several groups, and a few elderly people walking up and down or else round and round like me, in thick coats and with dogs on leads, and a woman in a dark green hat who tripped over her dog and almost fell. I called out as loudly as I could, but not loudly enough; the woman was too far away, a bus came by, passing between us. The swimming pool is always the same size and as the years go by you get to know exactly how loudly you need to call in order to be heard. Two girls were standing nearby, and when they giggled I knew that I had called out the wrong thing. The woman with her hat and dog had righted herself again. *Jumping in from the sides is strictly prohibited! Warning to non-swimmers!* In the Swimming Baths I know what to call out. Only the previous day I had still been there, though admittedly no one drowns in the bathtubs. The dirty water leaves a dark tidemark in the bath. It's important for bathers to shower before getting into the pool. A warning line of red tiles draws attention to the edge of the pool, because if anyone stumbles there they may fall into the water.

If you're concentrating on keeping a whole square in view you can easily bump into other pedestrians or a lamppost or telephone box. A man swore at me because he thought I was drunk, but that's not true. I did get drunk four nights running, but never at any other time. I crossed the road carefully so as to be closer to the square, but the woman was already out of sight and, as I moved on, part of the square was directly behind me so that I couldn't see anything any more. In the Swimming Baths it's a good idea to keep an eye on the red line, and if you follow it you can't go wrong.

As a lifeguard there's nothing for you to do in the street. The squares are too big, the streets are too noisy, and if you call out, you call out the wrong thing. I've been fired. But I've always left the house straight away in the mornings. First thing in the morning I would set out for the Baths. I know the way inside out, the places where puddles form when it rains, the smell of the buildings and the smell from the archways that lead into their yards, the sounds of heavy doors being swung open or shut, the hasty or weary steps, the lowered heads, sometimes even at that early hour a child running, as Tanja ran towards me from Cremer's kiosk, then a dog barking and straining at the leash, windows being opened and slammed shut. When I wake up all this sometimes comes back to me and I hear what I used to hear every morning until a few years ago. Since then the sounds have changed, there are more cars, the people look different, Tanja is long dead, and even the air isn't the same, but I've got used to that too, and sometimes I sit down on my bed in the boiler room, I'll be setting off in a minute, I think to myself, and then I remember that I'm already here.

On that first morning I kept asking people the time, because I couldn't ask the way and I had no watch. They looked at me impatiently, pointed to clocks on churches or other buildings and walked on, and I wished I could explain to them that I'm the lifeguard and that I'm not used to being out and about at this time of day, but nobody knew anything about the Swimming Baths or their closure, and no one recognized me.

Later on, when I told Cremer about losing my job, he shrugged and said I wasn't the only one, and anyway I should be glad, a few more years and you'd only have been able to walk round in a circle, even out in the street you'd have gone round in circles, he said.

"Anybody could work out the size of the pool by counting your paces," Cremer said, as though he'd been watching me.

I know it's not only in the swimming pool that disaster can strike. Cremer's daughter was run over in the street, and Cremer himself would sometimes read me snippets from the paper about calamities that had happened to other people, someone struck by lightning, another killed by a falling tile or branch—it comes to much the same thing in the end, but it's no concern of mine so long as they haven't drowned.

I would have liked to have turned back. Do you understand me? It was a fine day, fine weather, it wasn't raining, it was the right sort of day for a walk, but I would have liked to have turned back. The clothes that I was wearing had been adequate for the walk from the flat to the Swimming Baths. It's only a short way, I could do it in my sleep, and when once in a while it was cold and rainy it didn't matter too much because I'd soon be reaching the centrally heated Swimming Baths and could change out of my wet things.

My feet were sore, I'd have liked to have rested, but it was cold and I didn't know where to sit down. It's embarrassing to sit on a bench in full public view. I had no reason to be in the street. There's nothing for a lifeguard to do there. I'd have liked to have turned back, although I had lost my bearings, and no sooner had I discovered the right direction again, no sooner had I decided to go that way than it struck me that even in that direction I had no idea where I could go, and so I would turn round and, not wanting to end up too far away, walked round the sides of a large square as though it were the swimming pool.

I had to be vigilant, for there must always be someone to guard against a disaster occurring, I thought, and as long as you're doing that nothing can happen to you yourself, because it's absurd and inexcusable for the lifeguard to come to harm while taking care that none of the bathers drowns. But I found it impossible to remain alert and vigilant. The colors slither about from the cars and billboards and people's clothes on to other people and billboards or cars, everything moves fast, much faster than in a swimming pool. I longed for quiet, but there was such a shrieking of colors that in the end I raised my hands as I did at the baths when I called out: *Silence!* Do you hear me? There was too much noise. I stretched out my arms. To do this I had to stand still, and a man who was walking behind me bumped into me and hissed at me angrily, and I stood there with my arms outstretched, and my hands were red and numb with cold.

When I saw the man walking ahead of me, murmuring to himself, I was as startled as if it were someone I knew. He had a big hump on his shoulders, covered by a heavy gray overcoat from beneath which poked two checked trouser legs that were too short; on his skinny calves he wore one gray and one black sock, his shoes were too big, and when he stopped I saw that his neck was set crookedly between his rounded shoulders. He turned round and smiled, mumbling to himself, broke off, then started again as if he were trying to say something to me, and again I seemed to feel a shock of recognition, although I couldn't possibly have known him. He had never come to the Swimming Baths, I don't think you can swim with a hump, there are people who aren't hunchbacks and still can't swim, and I would have remembered a hunchbacked bather, because even if you don't know people by name you can see perfectly well how a person moves and whether he has a hump or not. Yet he smiled at me as though we knew each other, and because I was walking faster, he speeded up too, keeping in step with me as if he were my shadow, and I felt embarrassed because he was not fit company for a lifeguard, and if I talk to myself that's different, because what I say makes sense and anyone listening would have no difficulty in understanding me.

At one time cripples and invalids did occasionally come, and if they weren't dead I would be sure to recognize them, but that was long ago, which is why I assume they must be dead by now. As a child I was afraid of them because my father used to shout that I should be thankful that he was not a cripple although he too had been in the war, I should be grateful to him for it, and I *was* grateful that his hands were normal when he grabbed hold of me and shouted that I must never forget that. He decreed that I must do sport because I was such a slow runner and could never catch a ball. I hated ball games and so I went swimming, because otherwise I would have remained a weakling, little better than a cripple. Look at them, shouted my father, and his arms were healthy and strong, and he wanted to have nothing to do with cripples and idiots. In our family no one falls ill, he would say, threatening me, and I'd never miss either school or swimming. In our family no one was ill, neither my mother nor I, or even my father right up to the day when he hanged himself, and we had nothing to do with cripples and mad people. They would only rarely came to the Swimming Baths; by now they are dead and have vanished of their own accord, whereas in the past you used to see them in the streets on a Sunday when my father took us for a walk, on Sundays because on weekdays one didn't have the time, and unless one was going for a walk there was no point in aimlessly hanging around in the streets, since one was not a cripple or a madman or tramp. It was just about tolerable in the case of cripples because they had been in the war, as one could see from their legs having been blown off, when they sat on small boards propelling themselves around on wheels with their hands, if they still had any hands, and my father said that most of them were cowards and had brought their misfortune on themselves, for after all he had been in the war too and had come back unscathed. I was forbidden to speak to them, and I didn't, because as a child I was frightened of them and later on they never came to the Swimming Baths, because people who come to the baths have both arms and two legs, or at any rate one arm but always both legs. Blind people didn't come either, nor did mad people who talked aloud to themselves or laughed for no reason because, on the whole, people who go swimming are healthy and in their right mind.

Do you hear me? I don't know the people, I can't be blamed for that, and if some madman in the street thinks he knows me, I'm not responsible for that. Had he been trying to say something to me I couldn't have made it out because the traffic was too noisy. Do you understand? It's either very noisy or very quiet. On that day there was so much noise that I couldn't hear anything, a fine day, if a cold one, and the square was endless, although time seemed not to be passing at all, I would have liked to have turned back but went on and on until it got dark. Only then did I turn back and go to Cremer's kiosk.

I made an effort to keep to the proper times, to leave the house punctually in the morning and return at the usual time in the evening. The time in between was too long. I went out at the same time as always, and came back as always. That's what I was used to, and in the morning one does leave the house. I said nothing to my mother and nothing to Cremer. In the evening, when I got to his kiosk, he'd grumpily push the bag of rolls towards me, "Where have you been, they're dry now," he said, nothing more, I took the bag, nodded, said nothing. I've never been one to say much, and in the end you can't explain what you would like to explain, because surely everyone should know it by now— *The swimming pool is closed.* Those sentences are hung up like big placards or signs, everyone can see them, the sentences only repeat what's there before their eyes, and I never had a secret, there was a piece of white paper posted up at the entrance during the time when the individual baths were still open for use, *The Swimming Pool is closed*, it said, and soon afterwards the paper was replaced by a notice on a piece of cardboard. *As of 30 November, the People's Baths will be closed.* Everyone could see it.

I clearly remember the day after I lost my job. I spent it walking the streets of the city. Towards evening I saw a thin man who was sitting on a bench with his face in his hands who didn't look up when I stopped in front of him. He's asleep, I thought, sleeping in a public place, and I stopped, but he didn't move even when I called to him in quite a soft voice.

In the Swimming Baths none of the bathers knew my name, not even the regulars knew it. Since I was never called by my name they couldn't know what it was, nobody except Cremer used my name, and in the baths it was irrelevant since I was the lifeguard and there wasn't another, so they could simply call out, "Lifeguard!" and that would always be me. I didn't take much finding, I was always near the pool, or certainly no further away than the changing rooms, but generally I was walking round the pool and I could see when somebody was trying to call me. I tried always to be on the alert, because a person in the water may not have the time, or the strength, to call out loudly, and I did my best to ensure that no one would ever have to shout. No one should have to shout, I thought, I've always hated to hear anyone shout, it always bodes ill, whereas calling is something I like to hear, and the same goes for the children's shrieking, you can't imagine a swimming pool without it, the noise that children make is an intrinsic part of a swimming pool when children are there, but that isn't shouting, just the sound of high, clear voices, similar to the sound of people calling me:

"Lifeguard!" You out there—listen to me!

And then, from one day to the next, no one was calling me or using my name any more, only Cremer said, just a few more times, "Good morning, Hugo," and that was all, because I rarely spoke to my mother, she was asleep when I left the house and when I came back she was asleep, too, she slept a lot in those last few weeks, and before long she had died. On this particular day she was still alive, but we hardly spoke to one another, I didn't say a word to her nor she to me, that's all there was to it. Her hearing wasn't good, so she had told me, and perhaps this man sitting on the bench asleep was also hard of hearing, or else he was sleeping very deeply, but there are also people who die suddenly, even if it's rare for someone to die right there in the street. But you can never be sure, and perhaps this day was a day of ill-fortune, although no one said anything and they all walked on, ignoring the man, just as they had ignored me, apart from the man in the checked trousers who had stared at me and was crippled and possibly mad, who wore trousers that were too short, whereas the man on the bench was respectably dressed and had his head resting in his hands, which were on a small case placed next to him, and he didn't hear me. But then he began to snore, so it wasn't a day of ill-fortune, nothing had happened and nothing was happening on this day any more than on any other, and suddenly I thought that if this man were to wake up just now he would think I was mad, and I quickly walked on.

Anyone who isn't respectably dressed has no business to be out in the street, my father would say. If he saw any stains or a hole or missing buttons he would start to bellow, and since my fifteenth birthday I have never worn trousers that were too short. My mother always kept my clothes in good order, taking them from my room while I was at the baths, and buying anything I needed. We talked as little about that as about anything else. It seldom happened that we sat together in the living room or in the kitchen, only on days when the Baths were completely closed. Neither of us liked it, even though she used to complain about my not talking to her. You never tell me anything, she'd grumble, but there was nothing to tell, and she didn't want to hear about my work as a lifeguard. Her hearing was poor, in any case. Later, she was almost completely deaf, and because of this, when she went out she'd smile more than before, starting to smile even in the hallway.

"In case I don't quite catch what people say," she explained, "I smile, pretending to have heard. Everybody does that," she claimed, "what difference does it make?"

In the mornings I'd put the coffee on for her. What she did with herself all day long I don't know, for since my father's friends had stopped coming, no one visited her any more, and there wasn't much to do in the flat.

"Why should I visit anyone if nobody comes to see me?" she'd say, grumbling that not even her own son talked to her.

"If only your father had lived to see this," she said when the Wall came down, and then she urged me to go and speak to the authorities.

"Your father," she said, "was persecuted, perhaps they'll give you a job at last."

Often, when I came home, and she searched my clothes for stains, she'd say,

"Was für eine Schande! It's a disgrace!"

My clothes got very little wear, since for work I'd put on swimming trunks and a bathrobe and wore the shirts and trousers only for the walk between the baths and the flat, and the leather shoes also got hardly any wear because I never put them on, so that I didn't need much in the way of clothes, and what I did wear was impeccable.

If you keep yourself respectable nothing can happen to you. You'll be all right in the end, I thought. Anyone looking at you will see that it's all a mistake. A mistake is regrettable, and everything possible must be done to rectify it.

Now it doesn't matter any more. Anybody who jumps in from the side now will smash their skull on the tiles. The whole floor of the pool was smeared with blood, the old lifeguard told me, there were dead people lying there, and now that the pool is empty they're lying there again. At the end of the war, the old lifeguard said, they shot the prisoners. He lived in the building next door and soldiers came and forced him to open up, remove the corpses and clean up the pool. There were twelve of them, the old lifeguard said. Since the pool hall and the pool itself have been empty it's as if I can smell the stench rising up from between the tiles, and men come, men I don't know, they come into the pool area wearing boots, paying no heed to what I call out to them, and there are others who crouch naked on the floor of the empty pool or pace up and down like prisoners.

They are going to demolish the building. The whole city is full of building sites, as I've seen for myself, deep holes full of water with people climbing like insects up and down the sides, they have big helmets and building equipment, and above them mechanical diggers crawl along the edge as though bent upon filling in the hole and burying everything that moves inside it.

They had to use a pneumatic drill, Cremer told me, to dig a grave for his mother in the frozen earth. Because of that, he added, it cost us more than an ordinary burial. But if we'd waited, where could she have been kept in the meantime?

The pits are big enough for entire buildings to disappear

into them as though under a rock-fall or landslide which swallows up whatever was there before, and only a few days later everything looks as though it had always been like that.

Corpses rot and turn to water, the water seeps away, and if it doesn't seep away it collects in one place, and if you're digging and happen to strike a bubble of underground corpse water it spurts up like a fountain and anyone hit by it will die. Water from corpses is poisonous, dead bodies turn into poisonous water, Cremer read to me out of a magazine. They dissolve, and if a cemetery is designed for cheapness or is on an unsuitable site, the cemetery gardeners and gravediggers die like flies. It depends on the geological strata, Cremer read, and one drop of water from a corpse is enough to kill a living person. Whether the corpse drowned or hanged itself like my father makes no difference at all. I saw to the job of cutting him down, and then he was buried. I wasn't present at his burial. He should have been burnt. The fact that he had died didn't do me any good. On the globe there's more water than land, and even where there is land, there's water to be found beneath it. When he died I looked at the globe, picking out the countries I would travel to. But the water predominates, it has won.

When I moved about in the flat my mother would watch to see that I didn't make any dirty marks, my father would send me outside and I had to make sure that there was not a leaf, not a bit of dirt, not a scratch on my shoes when I came back, my mother used to follow at my heels checking that I wasn't leaving any footprints, she'd send me to my room. Then as soon as my father arrived home, he'd call and when I came out of the room he'd box my ears and ask me what I'd been doing in my room. I was never on my own at home; my door was not to be shut and my mother made sure that it never was. That boy spends all his time skulking indoors, my father would bellow and pack me off outside. I went on wearing my trousers until they were way above my ankles, but my shoes were always new. The other children hid when they saw me, they threw dirt at me, leaves, stones, taunted me because I avoided parks and other places where there was dirt, where I would scuff my shoes on bushes and stones, just look at your shoes, my father bellowed. I wasn't allowed to enter my room with shoes on, I had to leave them by the front door, and when he came home the first thing he did was to check the state of my shoes, then he'd come down the hallway and was there in my room and he'd snatch the books out of my hands.

"A cry-baby pussyfoot! Nothing to say for himself! Always skulking indoors!" he'd bellow when he saw me working at my books. I never saw him unshaven. He always wore a shirt and one of his three ties. Above his shirt, his face was smooth, you only saw his skin above the buttoned-up collar, and when he shouted his face turned red as if he were about to choke.

He'd snatch the books from my hands, demanding to see my homework. If he couldn't find anything to criticize, he'd be annoyed. Then, he'd call my mother, what does the boy do all day, he'd demand to know, gripping me by the shoulders, why does he sit around in his room all day?

Until I was fifteen years old I'd wear trousers that were too short, they didn't reach down to my ankles, and my socks were meticulously checked for holes every week. I had to darn the holes myself, Father was stingy about socks and trousers.

"Here he comes with his trousers at half mast!" the others would call out when they saw me, closing in around me and stamping on my shoes, which were always new and always made of good stout leather that shone, for we had good footwear in abundance—my father had a whole collection which he stored in the cellar, I wasn't supposed to know that, there must have been shoes of every size there, as good as new, my father loved good footwear, they stood lined up in some old cupboards in the cellar, I didn't know where they came from, and after his death my mother secretly threw them away.

It's forbidden to enter the pool area wearing shoes. It's strictly forbidden to approach the pool in outdoor shoes. You don't know what sticks to shoes, it's often something bad, and one must at all costs prevent it from coming into contact with the water. I saw most of the people barefoot. Often their feet are ugly, covered in corns and calluses, as ugly as their bodies— thick toes, crooked toes, flat feet and thick ankles, the skin as pale as if the feet were destined to die first, as if the blue veins were inscriptions marking the grave or recording the manner of death or a misdeed, with yellow toenails curving and growing into the flesh, but that's still better than shoes. A lifeguard wears beach sandals at work, and even in winter I used to walk to the Swimming Baths in trainers, which soaked up water and easily got dirty, so I kept another pair at the Swimming Baths because I didn't want to walk through the changing rooms in the dirty shoes, and certainly not along the edge of the pool, where in any case beach sandals are preferable because if someone is drowning you have to jump into the water quickly, and leather shoes are not at all suitable. No bather has ever been rescued by someone with leather shoes on.

Chapter four

Three days ago a chunk of plaster broke away from the wall. When I came into the pool area this morning I saw, under the stand, the fragments which I had swept up and carried down to the basement to take out to the dustbins after dark. There's no cause for alarm, I thought to myself, in the dim light it's easy to be mistaken. I raised my head and saw the lions above me. The outermost lion had lost a paw.

It must have broken off during the night or first thing this morning. The stone is giving way.

The noise you can hear now comes from outside. I've been up to the gallery to look out of the window. The road has been torn up, the building on the far side is encased in scaffolding, and over the scaffolding there's a green tarpaulin cover. A short while ago a man was dangling from the guttering as though he had hanged himself. The wind was making him sway to and fro, and I was on the point of running outside to fetch help. But then he raised his arm and swung a hammer against the front of the building.

The house where my parents live is only a few streets further on, and they're both dead. You people can do whatever you like with that house, I shan't go back there. In the bathroom there's a pink runner. I threw the hair curlers away. What happened to the rope I don't know.

"Wanted a dance with the rope maker's daughter, did he?" a neighbor called out to me on the stairs after the police had left. I was carrying my swimming things.

I'd vowed to myself that as soon as I'd done my school-leaving exams I would move out, go to university and never come back to my parents' flat. When I heard my father's footsteps in the hall, I try to hide my book, but he snatched it out of my hand and slammed it shut, I had bruises, it was only when I took up swimming that he began to be more careful, when I undressed the others laughed, we were all naked, I swam as fast as I could. I would move out straight away, I promised myself, away from those three rooms, the long hallway, my room at the end of it. We ate in the kitchen.

"It's a disgrace—eine Schande!" my father would say, but he didn't say why. A bunch of cowards, he'd rage, and my mother would nod nervously.

"What's the boy been doing today?" he would ask my mother, "What do you want to do, learn history?" he jeered, "Do you know what lies are? They would have shown you what's what, and this is supposed to be my son, sticks his head in his books and can't even look me in the face, what are you staring at me like that for?"

I'd hear the footsteps in the passage, at once felt his eyes on me, pale eyes watching me, curious, as if waiting to see whether I'd fall down, as though I'd been made to stand there, was standing there in a row with some others, that's how I stood before him, as though at any moment he might send me plunging down, into what, I didn't know.

Seized hold of me, dragged me into the bathroom, in front of the mirror, beat me with his belt in front of the mirror, "Bend over the bath!" he barked, "Here!" he forced my head round to look into the mirror and boxed my ears, I saw the naked body in the mirror, saw my face.

When my father was buried I didn't go to the funeral; I sat in my room, he wouldn't be tearing open the door, wouldn't be snatching the book from my hand and taking it away from me. I didn't need to hide anything, a book under the blanket, my face, my shoes and where I'd been in them. I thought I would die, my father had hanged himself, I had heard the rumor, a classmate repeated it to me, what father did—shot children dead, and every day the other boys at school would come up to me, he'd shot them in a pit, the girls wouldn't speak to me, they ran away when I came anywhere near them, shot them dead, said the boys, and I saw his eyes before me, my mother had closed them, she had very quickly become quite calm as though she were relieved. It was only three days later when I refused to go to the funeral with her, that she shouted. She shouted at me for the first time ever, and as I stood my ground and didn't give in to her I was thinking: No. No one could do anything to me now.

"The Swimming Baths have been closed. I've been fired."

"You're not the only one," Cremer said.

A green tarpaulin covers the building opposite. At first I thought it was being renovated, now I'm not so sure. They haven't set up a crane or brought any containers. Perhaps they're going to blow it up, or gut it, leaving the foundations and the frontage and pulling down the rest. For three weeks I wandered around the city. The streets change within the space of a week, before you know it you're walking through a no-man's-land, all at once a whole terrace of houses has gone and only the bare fire walls rear up above craters, pieces of wasteland strewn with battered household items, nettles growing up among them, there are smashed cupboards, washing machines, television sets lying about, broken windows and above them some roof tiles, here and there a door hangs above the void, the inside of a flat with wallpaper and water pipes.

Carried on walking through the streets, often getting lost, I didn't recognize the streets, from one day to the next I didn't know whether I'd been there before or not, even buildings that I must have seen before I didn't recognize, the buildings are being pulled down or covered in scaffolding, I thought, the windows torn out, the occupants are moving away, and I forgot that I hadn't known them. In front of the driveway leading into a courtyard I found dried-out pot plants, broken crockery, a box full of letters. They're all on the point of leaving, I thought, they're going away from here, looking for work elsewhere, moving a few streets away or out of the city altogether.

No one will say anything if they blow up the People's Baths. The building has stood here for almost a hundred years, the wrought ironwork with the fish design, the flowers clambering up the pillars to the gallery, the arches, the turquoise tiles with their varied coloration, the shell-shaped niche at the top end.

I will not let myself be driven out. It was my responsibility to see that nobody drowned. Nobody did drown.

There were spiders before. But now they've multiplied, they've lost all fear, their webs are everywhere, as tightly woven as the green tarpaulin opposite, like an airtight cover on a jar. Of the two flights of stairs from the back end of the pool up to the gallery, the right-hand one is smothered in cobwebs as thick as if they were meant to trap a human being. When I walk into one of these webs I touch my face and hair, there are threads sticking to my eyelashes or my clothes, then I feel revulsion and I try to remove them from the stairway, from the doors, but, overnight, fresh webs appear and the spiders are clever at keeping out of sight.

In the night, I sometimes think to myself, in the night while I'm asleep in the boiler room—who knows what will happen when I'm no longer here at all?

It won't be long now. Can anyone hear what I'm saying? Up here around the pool there are microphones in place. At night when no one was here, that's when the caretaker must have let the men in to install them. The microphones pick up anything that's said, every word is recorded. There used to be all the other voices, children shouting, people calling out, the splash when someone jumped in. *Jumping in from the sides is strictly prohibited!* Can anybody hear me? A paw broke off the outermost lion last night. But I'm not leaving here any more.

On Sundays we used to go for a walk, right up to the end. We'd have lunch, then the walk. My mother, my father, and me behind them.

For my fifteenth birthday I was given two pairs of trousers.

"Your mother tells me that you go out of the house in your old trousers!"

No more going out in trousers that were too short, ever again. My shoes were also checked when I came home. Scratches. The soles. The heels.

"Where do you hang around anyway?"

When it was warm enough I would take a book, steal out

of the flat, go to the park. The walk from the house to the park and back. Always by the shortest route. The Swimming Baths three times a week. We did training every day, I lied, and set out with my swimming kit, and if it was raining I went and sat in an underground station. To school every morning. On Sundays, my parents' backs in front of me on our walk.

Sirens and more sirens, squealing brakes, people crossing the road whenever and wherever they please, car horns hooting, no warning calls, and instead the street signs, traffic lights . . . who could possibly keep proper watch over all these people? Sirens and more sirens and sparks from the tram wires, and behind the cars the billboards, cars at a standstill one behind another, gleaming metal, music pounding out even through the car windows, pedestrians in among the cars, no one calling out a warning, the big carrier bags with words printed on them, the glass doors, and people's steps disappearing into the bright light.

"Where've you been?" Cremer asked me on the evening of the first day.

"You look rough!" he said but pushed the bag with the rolls in my direction and didn't pursue it further. He thought I was still in charge of the bath cubicles, didn't know I'd been dismissed or that the Baths had been closed down. It was evening and had been dark for a long time, nearly time to go back to the flat as on any other day. This was the first day, in the morning it had been fine, now it was starting to rain, I'd hardly finished eating the rolls when it started to rain, and although I was tired and very close to the street where we lived I found it hard to go there, I was thinking of the evenings with the others, with Klaus, Frau Karpfe and the caretaker. All day long I hadn't seen a familiar face, I hadn't seen anybody except the man with the checked trousers, I'd seen the thin man sitting on the bench with a rucksack on his back, and no one had spoken to me.

I didn't go straight back to the flat, I made a detour and

went to the Swimming Baths. At first I thought I saw a light, but the windows were dark, I saw the white notice announcing the permanent closure of the baths, I was about to go up the steps to read it, but a car braked and parked right in front of the building, a man got out and eyed me curiously, and I turned and went away. In all the other windows lights could be seen, only at the People's Baths and Swimming Pool was it dark, and in the murky haze that hung about the buildings it looked as if where the Baths stood there was nothing but an empty space.

The pool is empty, I stare into it for hours on end until I do see something, a swimmer doing back crawl, his straight arms reaching out of the water, his face upturned towards the ceiling, his feet kicking in a fast and even rhythm, I see another diving under, touching the edge of the pool and smoothly pushing himself off, I hear someone doing a front crawl, taking noisy breaths, and I wait for them all to get safely out of the water, I'd give them a towel if they haven't got one, in the basement there are towels in the locker, towels and swimming trunks and two plastic boats which children have left behind.

It started to rain. I'd been fired on the previous day. I'd spent the whole day walking around in the city. Before, I'd never needed a raincoat or an umbrella: I knew I'd soon be there. For the first time I had not been there, at the Swimming Baths, and when I went up the stairs to the flat I paused on the landing, the light went out, and there was not a sound to be heard.

As I entered the flat I heard voices and could see the glow of the television in the living room. On this day, as on those that followed, I didn't speak to my mother, I went straight to my room and fell asleep at once.

In the morning I woke up, still fully dressed. I was afraid to get up, I had fallen asleep in my clothes, and the clothes were stiff as though they were reluctant to move. It made me think of the plaster cast on Cremer's leg. Cremer had had a fall and couldn't get up by himself, and because I was at the kiosk, I helped him up and went with him to the hospital, this was three or perhaps four years ago, and since then he has walked with a limp. Someone had to pick him up, he couldn't get back on to his feet by himself, and even that was no use since one leg was broken. Now it's just as if he'd always had a limp and as if that were his reason for having the kiosk, where he stays sitting on one spot from morning till night, as the kiosk is so small that you can't move in it. Cremer limps, getting around is difficult for him, but he never used to walk much, he'd fallen down in front of his kiosk, and when the ambulance came it made him think of his daughter and he started to cry, he was in pain too because his leg was broken, and then the leg was put in plaster and he couldn't move it. The kiosk stayed shut for a week, and Cremer stayed at home and I visited him there in the evenings, his wife opened the door, she always opened the door as if it just might be her daughter, eyes bright in her thin face, and then she looked at me, gave a friendly nod and took me through to the living room, where Cremer was lying on the sofa in front of the television, and on it were silver-framed photographs of Tanja.

They were stiff with dirt, the clothes I had slept in, it was still dark, raining, the days misty like a web of fine threads that gradually expands and smothers everything, smothers the light. I'd have a shower at the Swimming Baths, I thought, take my clothes off; important notice: *Bathing costume or swimming trunks must be removed while the body is cleansed. Thorough cleansing is required before the pool may be used. Any visit to the lavatory must be made before the body is cleansed.* It was high time I set out. I'd have a shower at the Swimming Baths, I thought, as I still didn't want to use the bathroom in the flat, I left the house without having had a cup of tea and went in the wrong direction straight away, not wanting to say good morning to Cremer, not wanting anybody to recognize me, it was still dark, I hadn't got undressed or dressed again while my body was being cleansed, he talks to himself, they had scoffed, and the man with the checked trousers whom I had seen the day before was also still talking to himself continuously, the notices, the warning signs aren't there, soon I would have forgotten what they said, everything is forgotten in the end, the Swimming Baths were closed and no one stopped me to say: "They've closed the Swimming Baths."

Buildings are being demolished, blown up, I've seen that myself. The bathers have stopped coming, the walls are decaying, I'd gone in the wrong direction, I'd be late, soon people would be able to tell just by looking at me, my shoes scuffed, trousers too short, above my ankles, cripples who talk aloud to themselves, wander the streets, sit on the benches, dirty, shabby, people with broken skin or rashes aren't allowed to use the pool.

People with broken skin and rashes are excluded from using the pool, people who talk aloud to themselves, all these people must be excluded because people using the streets have a right to be spared such things, broken skin and rashes, that's easy to remember, dirty and scuffed shoes, disgraceful, types who just hang around, who skulk indoors. On Sundays you go for a walk, on a Sunday, anyone who doesn't work doesn't deserve to eat, I had never been ill in all those years, and never late, now I went in the wrong direction, the days were far too long, it was the first day, then the second day; then it was days, days like every day, as though it had always been like this, it slowly grew light, it was raining, I thought I should turn back, at the Baths it was always warm, I'd have a shower there. I had avoided using my mother's bathroom for a long time, her pink hair curlers lay around there and sometimes underwear, the smell of eau-de-Cologne clung to the towels, eau-de-Cologne and hair spray, a smell which filled me with revulsion in the same way as the naked, ageing bodies, the flabby backs, wrinkled ankles, thick blue veins on feet, the brown spots that come with age, or the birthmarks. But in the pool they're all the same, in the water any difference disappears, the odor is absorbed into the water and remains there, without thorough cleansing the pool may not be used, and people with broken skin and rashes are excluded from using the Baths; but all others have access at any time, from six in the morning to nine at night, the time dragged, I never used to be aware of time.

In the streets there's no one checking who has a right to be there and who hasn't, anyone can stay in the street for as long as he likes, there's no one responsible for keeping order or making sure that nothing happens to anybody, people rush this way and that, they're in a hurry, and other people get in their way and under their feet so that they could easily trip or fall, and all around there's so much noise that nobody pays any attention. Every day people disappear without anyone noticing, just as I am no longer at the place where I live, nor at my place of work now that I no longer work because the Swimming Baths are closed, and when you disappear it has no consequences. There may be people walking about in the streets who have in fact disappeared. It's not easy to establish a thing like that, just as one can't say anything definite about the people who don't come to the Baths, who are not all excluded from using the pool but stay away for quite different reasons, like Cremer or my mother for instance, neither of whom had any broken skin, or any rashes.

Sometimes I wake up in the night and don't immediately know where I am. The Swimming Baths are not a place for sleeping in, and when I wake up I don't naturally assume that I'm at the Baths. But now that I've got my globe back and found three more, which I leave on at night, I feel calmer, because in my room at home I always had the globe switched on at night, until one morning my mother came to wake me because I had failed to wake up of my own accord, and put it by the door. I was to throw it away because the borders on it weren't right any more and it wasn't a good thing for a globe like that to be found in the house.

Now the lights in two of the globes have gone, and when I feel a shock of alarm on waking up I wonder whether this is right and I really am here, whether I really did have to go wandering around the city because the Swimming Baths have been closed down, and sometimes it seems as if it must all be an invention, in the way that a dream is an invention, because when all's said and done it's unthinkable that they would let a whole building fall into decay, that walls not be walls but become mere iron struts, straw and mortar; just as a swimming pool without water, a swimming pool hall in which the water has been turned off, is also unthinkable.

In the boiler room I wake up and can't rule out the possibility that I was the boiler man and not the lifeguard.

Cremer accused me of not knowing where I live, of having no idea of what was going on, and was annoyed because I wouldn't go with him when the Wall came down.

"Don't you understand," he said to me, "it's only a couple of hundred yards from your Swimming Baths, is it possible you've never actually seen the Wall? You don't think anybody's going to go swimming today, do you?"

But it wasn't true. Most of the bathers did come, it was just a little quieter than usual in the pool area, while one could hear the sound of people talking loudly both from outside and from Frau Karpfe's office. The people who had come swam just as usual, if anything they stayed in the water for longer, I remember that, they stayed a long time, doing their lengths, as if they couldn't make up their minds to leave the pool, and when they had stopped they hung on to the side rails, until the water had settled down again as though nothing had happened, as though they were not there. Hung there quietly unmoving, holding the handrails in the water, each one separate, not talking to one other, whereas in the preceding weeks it had been noisier than usual, but on this day it was so quiet that I didn't know whether to watch or not, and in the end I began to feel anxious that someone might be silently drowning without my noticing it.

Cremer shook his head about me, and my mother said that now everything would be different, I would surely get a job at last, mistakes would be cleared up, she said, pointing towards the living room as though my father were still hanging there. My mother was excited, she asked me why I still carried on going to those wretched Baths. When I got home at night she was waiting at the door for me; I said I was tired. I've always gone to bed early. Turned the light off straight away and got into bed, leaving only the light of the globe switched on. Nothing changed at the Baths. The People's Baths have existed for almost a hundred years. Even if the bathers who come now are different people and look different, they can still drown just the same.

It was wrong of her to take the globe and put it by the door for throwing out. It wasn't doing any harm in the room. A globe isn't big. It doesn't take up much space, and whether the borders are right or not is irrelevant.

"That mustn't be found here," she said, as though the flat

were in danger of being searched and things might be found that would be compromising.

"Times have changed," she insisted.

I had overslept that day and was afraid of being late, I wasn't drunk, the others hadn't taken me along with them, they probably sat together until late as they had on the previous evenings, and I waited for a while to see whether they would come back, whether Klaus would come back and fetch me. At night I had always gone straight home to sleep so as to be up on time in the morning, and I went straight to bed—I'd long since given up reading, the books had been cleared out—leaving only the light of the globe switched on, it's very dark at night and the globe has a blue light, it's standing in the boiler room next to the others which I found later, their light too dim to be noticed from outside, and I sleep more peacefully with the light there, I'm alone in the whole building, there's no one else here and nothing to be heard but the rustling and squeaking of the mice and the fluttering and high piping cries of the bats that roost in the corridor between the basement and the pool hall. It's the wrong time of year, they ought to be hibernating, they've no business to be in a swimming bath at all, but the light of the globes will keep them away, and when I wake up I know where I am.

During those days I didn't see my mother, although I came home earlier than usual. I went straight to bed and slept, not looking to see whether she was still awake or not, it was only later that I tried to think whether I had noticed the light of the television, whether she had been sitting in the living room. Perhaps she was already lying in her bed, ill. I was trying to avoid her. She would have asked me why I had suddenly started wearing the outdoor shoes and the heavy coat, I had never put either of them on before, since it wasn't far to the Swimming Baths and

I got undressed as soon as I arrived there, but now I was walking around out of doors all day, all day in shoes, coat and beneath it a pullover and shirt, and perhaps no one recognized me because no one knew me in those clothes, just as I was unused to seeing people only when they were dressed.

I shan't go outside again. I don't like going outside. It's not that I have a bad conscience. I haven't done anything. I don't know the people outside. No one seems to be aware that the Swimming Baths have been closed. I haven't done anything, and I don't want to stay out in the streets. Again I saw the man with the checked trousers that were too short. There are people who spend their days in the city streets and on the benches at bus stops or in parks. I have always worked. I hardly ever went into town. I didn't need many things, and my mother always mended my swimming trunks and bathrobes. She bought me new trainers, I never wore the leather outdoor shoes. I never looked after them, but my shirts and pullovers are as good as new. I always looked respectable. No one can say that I let myself go. After my mother died I washed my own clothes. I pay the rent on time even though I don't set foot in the flat any more. I have always done what was right and proper.

I don't know the people out there, or the big streets, when I walk about I get lost, and when you walk in residential areas you can easily be taken for a thief or a tramp. If you are asked where you're going you don't know how to reply. One evening some policemen stopped me and asked where I was trying to get to. I had been walking up and down in front of a building, they asked me if I had some business there, and when I didn't know what to say they told me to go home.

After my mother died I could have stayed in the flat during the day, I did stay there for one whole day without going out,

I stood at the window and saw it was raining, it stayed very dark all day, in the house opposite they put the lights on at three o'clock, and I thought of the blue light of the globe and of how glad I would once have been to stay here, alone in my room all day with nobody making me go out or snatching the books from my hands: how long ago that was. In the room there's a bed, a table, at night I hung my clothes over the chair, and I had no use for the table, my mother put my clean clothes on it, she did the housework herself until she died, years ago she packed the books up in a box for me to take downstairs, then she dusted the bookcase. There would have been room for them in the basement, the flat is heated by gas, not coal, we don't need to use the basement for coal, and she never wanted any strangers in the flat, even to come and clean, and she was angry when I suggested it.

Cremer and his wife were the first strangers that I saw in the flat after her death; they were followed by the doctor and the undertaker's men, and when they had all gone I went into my room, closed the door behind me and stood at the window, without the light switched on, looking out at the windows of the other houses nearby. I could buy a newspaper from Cremer tomorrow, I thought, and I stayed at home for one whole day. Next day, after waking at the normal time, I went out, heading in the opposite direction from usual, and I have never spoken to Cremer since.

In the basement it's dusty, the coal dust gets into your mouth, and my eyes are stinging. Where should I have gone? Other people know where they're going, they go around in twos or threes, talking quietly together, it's obvious that nothing will happen to them, and a lifeguard is completely superfluous where there's no water and no swimming pool.

It was three weeks later, or four.

"Do you want to keep the life-belt as a souvenir?" the caretaker jeered. Can you hear me? I've spent my whole life making sure that no one drowns. I know my way about in the Swimming Baths but not in the streets. There's nothing for me to do there. I looked at people's faces and said nothing to anybody; the days were empty, it takes a long time for a day to pass.

Evenings, I would come home at my usual time, the flat was dark, from below, from the street I could see that there was no light on. It's the right-hand flat on the third floor, and slowly I climbed the stairs as if I didn't know that my mother was dead, wondering if she had gone shopping or to the hairdresser's, because my mother had no other reasons to leave the house. What she did during the day I don't know, she kept the flat and our clothes clean. When she complained that her legs hurt, I suggested getting a cleaning woman.

"My legs hurt," she kept complaining, but she wouldn't agree to have a stranger in the house, a cleaner, she said, that's all I need. She tried to show me her knees—"How am I supposed to do the housework with knees like this?" she'd ask me accusingly, but she rejected my suggestion of having one of the cleaners from the Baths.

"You've got no money!" she snapped at me, although she knew it was a lie.

In the end I got sick of hearing about it. In the mornings I would put her coffee on and leave; in the evenings, I let myself in quietly so that she shouldn't hear me. I didn't want to see her. She was almost eighty, at that age people die for no particular reason; that's nothing to do with me. The doctor said that she had taken sleeping tablets, perhaps too many, he found an empty packet on her bedside table.

"Has she been unhappy?" he asked, eyeing me suspiciously. I couldn't answer that, nor did I know where she had got sleeping tablets from, and he wouldn't believe me when I said that we hardly spoke to one another.

From below, from down in the street I looked up at the building, I didn't normally do that, the light was always on, where else would she be? The bluish light of the television in the living room, no light in my room, she demanded that I should throw the globe into the dustbin, I took it to the Baths and asked Klaus to look after it for me. I missed its light at night. Perhaps she couldn't sleep and that was why she had sleeping tablets, my mother's sleep is none of my business, and I never went into her bedroom except on that evening. I was surprised that it was dark, I called out from the hall and got no answer, so I opened the door to her room and switched the light on, she was lying in her bed, not moving, and when I touched her she was cold.

It was my job was to ensure that no one drowned. In all those years not one person drowned, but I had to reckon with that kind of death, drowning was the death that I had to think of. When Cremer's daughter had her fatal accident and I picked her up she was still warm. I would never have allowed her to drown. I was the one who taught her to swim. In the pool she was safe, and if on that afternoon she had not been playing in the street but in the pool as usual, she would still be alive. A lorry ran over her and killed her, not far from Cremer's kiosk, and when we ran across to her she was still warm. Dead people are not cold, I thought in wonderment. I held her in my arms, it was no effort to carry her, she weighed very little. Until the ambulance came I held her in my arms, because Cremer was shaking, he started shaking, since then it has turned into a twitching, his hands jerk when he reaches out. He would have dropped her.

But in the end all dead people are cold, I knew that from my father. It has nothing to do with drowning. Even so, I was surprised at how cold my mother's body was. She never went to the Swimming Baths, she didn't even like to hear them mentioned. It struck me that she could just as well be lying dead in the water, she was so cold, and then I went to Cremer, who is our neighbor. Her death is nothing to do with me, as I explained to the doctor, whom Cremer had phoned and who gave me an odd look because I couldn't say where I had been that day. And Cremer said I should have her buried, he didn't go to the kiosk the next day and did everything that had to be done, for which I am grateful to him.

Cremer's eyes, too, were full of suspicion, he asked me what I had been doing for the past few days, and I explained to him that the Baths were closed and that I'd lost my job, explained to him that I'd been wandering around the city and that there was nothing more I could say. He shook his head, and when I raised no objection to the undertaker's suggestion that my mother should be cremated, he asked me if I'd taken leave of my senses.

"An anonymous urn and no ceremony?! You want to have her cremated?" he asked in horror. But I was thinking of the corpse water, he had told me himself that dead people emit corpse water.

At noon they came to collect my mother. In the evening Cremer and his wife came round, bringing me bread and milk and cheese, and when they had gone I stripped my mother's bed, then closed the bedroom door behind me, as I have no use for that room. There were once three of us living there, then two, now the flat is standing empty. I went back a few times to fetch things that I needed, a kettle and clean clothes, and each time I was afraid of being waylaid by one of the neighbors or by Cremer.

Four days ago I wanted to go into the flat again. I unlocked the front door to the building and climbed the stairs. The door of the flat had been sealed up. I stood in front of the door, the key to which is legitimately in my possession. I thought that this was where I was officially supposed to be, whereas in the Swimming Baths I'm trespassing. From the landing I could hear the neighbors on the floor below. I was about to call out to them when they started talking about me and about how there was no trace of me.

"He's disappeared," said one neighbor, just as though he'd never existed."

"Vanished without trace," the other agreed, "you'd think he'd never lived here."

"If a whole Wall can disappear," said the first, "so can a person."

"He was out of work anyway," said the other. "What a good thing his mother isn't alive to see this."

I waited until the two neighbors had gone into their flats and closed the doors, then I went, unobserved by anyone, down the stairs and out of the building, and as I walked down the street I thought about the fact that I'd vanished without trace, and hoped that I wouldn't meet anyone who knew me. But I've no need to worry on that score. The people who have seen me as a lifeguard wouldn't recognize me, they only know me in swimming trunks or a bathrobe and for them, as for myself, I existed where my place had been all my life, in the Baths, by the side of the pool.

No one would have prevented me from staying in the flat. If I had not woken up at the normal time no one would have noticed, I could have spent the whole day there and all the following days too, and I did actually stay at home for one day; first I wandered through the passage and the living room and into the kitchen. In the bathroom my mother's curlers were lying around and I gathered them up and then went down and took them to the dustbin, together with her bedding. I have nothing to hide. The bedding wasn't clean; the doctor asked me if we had had a good relationship, I answered that we had both lived here and nothing in particular had ever happened. Cremer explained that my father had killed himself, and when the doctor asked me where I worked I replied that I had been fired.

As for my mother's room, I only went in there to check whether she actually was lying there dead, and then once more when I got rid of the bedding. The flat was always tidy and clean, in the living room there were a sofa and two armchairs around a table, in the corner was the television and on the television the photograph of my father. I considered putting his photo away but didn't know where, and in the end I laid it face down on the table. In the cupboard I found a photograph album; the dates under the pictures had been crossed out. I threw the album away. Now, when I think of the flat and the fact that it's sealed, it seems to me that I should have thrown my father's photo away too. I shan't be going back. Three of us lived there, and now that I'm officially a missing person it's standing empty. But even in the days before that there was nobody there. I walked along the passage. I thought that now I could stay there during the day. The passage and all the rooms had linoleum on the floors, and you can hear when anyone walks on it. I kept walking about, sometimes stopping for a while at the window. It was the morning after they had taken my mother away, in a simple coffin which would be cremated in two days' time, as the two men explained to me in a manner that suggested I had committed some error. It was very quiet; it was raining. I stood at the window for a long time. Just for a moment I thought I could hear my own footsteps, in the passage, in the living room, up and down.

It was on the day of my mother's cremation that I first went down and sat on the platform. It was raining, the last few leaves were falling from the trees, I was very soon wet through and chilled to the marrow, I had never been ill, I needed to sit down because I felt dizzy, in the Swimming Baths it was always warm, and you don't walk about in the streets for no reason. When I saw the underground sign I went down the steps, thinking that that would be somewhere to sit down. It was raining. As a boy I would sometimes go and sit in an underground station to read.

I wasn't depriving anyone else of a seat, there were not many people there, and most of those weren't sitting down but remained standing, knowing that they wouldn't have long to wait. Also it's draughty there. I saw the trains, the faces behind the big windows, the doors and the red light that blinks as a warning, each train is individually announced and each time a warning is called out, telling people to stand back; for a moment I wanted to get on a train and let it take me somewhere, but of course I didn't need to go anywhere. You can tell when someone isn't going anywhere.

Later on, some policemen came along with dogs on leads and took a good look at me, one dog came right up to me and sniffed at my legs through the muzzle it was wearing, I wanted to stand up but didn't want to go back to the flat, so I stayed sitting down, and when the officers finally moved away I felt that I must get back to the Swimming Baths at all costs.

During the morning whole school classes came, children with satchels and cases came racing down the steps, and their boisterous movements, close to the edge of the platform, filled me with anxiety. I have watched the platform attendants in their little glass booths, seen them chatting or reading, they are often not paying attention to what's happening on their platform, and for a while I thought it would be a good thing if I stayed there, I could keep an eye on one platform, because sometimes two trains arrive simultaneously and the platform attendant can't possibly watch the platforms on both sides at once, even if he comes out of his little box and stands right in the middle. He's in need of help, I thought, and I'm familiar with this kind of work and could offer him my help: I have a great deal of experience, I would tell him, in watching to see that no disaster occurs. No accident ever happened while I was on duty, not once in almost forty years, and the only reason I've been retired is that the Swimming Baths have been shut down, it's early retirement, I'm only fifty-eight.

For the next few days I spent each afternoon on an underground platform, at different stations and with different staff on duty; sometimes the platform was in the middle, in between the two lines, sometimes the platforms were on the left and right, with the line in each direction having its own separate platform. On one occasion a thin young man was sitting on a bench holding his face in both hands. I couldn't see his face, but I recognized him by his posture: it's something I'm very experienced at, recognizing people by their posture; it was three weeks, or four, since I'd seen him and his clothes had been quite respectable then, not like those of the hunchback with the checked trousers which only stretched up to his ankles, revealing socks that didn't match. It was the same young man I had seen on the day after my dismissal, so weary that he'd fallen asleep on a bench and didn't hear when I called to him, and then I saw that his clothes were dirty, torn, as though he'd been sleeping rough ever since, at bus stops or even in parks, and where his trouser leg was torn I could see that the cold had caused the skin on his bare leg to crack open, the wound was inflamed, and I thought that he mustn't be allowed into the Swimming Baths like that.

As far as possible I tried to avoid going to the same underground station more than once, and if I failed it was because my sense of direction went wrong. All the same, I did my best not to get in anyone's way. But it had turned cold and each day was as gray as the last, always the same dark morning when I woke up, and I resolved to wait until it was light, stood at the window, walked along the passage and into the kitchen, made myself some tea, and even after I had drunk the tea no time had passed. Every morning I thought that I ought to stay in the flat and that I'd get used to it, after all there was no reason to go out. "Be glad you're done with it," Cremer had said. And then I would go and get my coat after all, before it had got light, because on a normal day I'd have been late for work.

If you keep walking all day long your feet ache, you need to sit down and rest, your eyes get tired, you can easily stumble, people look at you in the street, sometimes two of them put their heads together, whispering, and perhaps I was speaking aloud to myself at times. People walk by, you see their faces behind the car windows, behind the big shop windows or the windows of houses, there are very many of them, I wouldn't be able to remember any individual face, and I recognized nobody. The light was too bright for me despite the overcast sky, you can't cope with the brightness, everybody can see you in the street, and I spent more and more time down in the underground stations, which are often almost empty, you can have a rest there without disturbing anyone, and when the trains come you have to watch to ensure that no one falls on to the rails and is run over.

The platform staff on the underground stations would find me useful, I thought; four eyes are better than two, and I did eventually offer them my help, but no one was interested, although I enquired repeatedly and always politely, not begging. I receive a pension and I don't need charity.

They laughed at me. Behind the glass I would see a face, a shake of the head, I couldn't hear the laughter because all they had to do was to close the little window. You stand in front of it like a petitioner, although I've never asked for anything in my life unless you count the chlorine and flocculent, but they were not for me, they were essential for the quality of the water.

The third man I asked became abusive and threatened to summon the police. They patrol up and down with their dogs, and if you sit on a bench for too long without getting on a train they ask you what you're doing there and whether you have nothing better to do, and once they demanded to see my identity card.

I have a clean record, and anyone who says differently is lying. I worked just like everyone else, I never missed a day; I did the work of two, and if the Swimming Baths are decaying it is not my fault.

My shoes are scuffed, because sometimes there's a crush of people or someone stumbles, or there's a stone on the pavement, and when it rains, water from the road splashes your coat and trousers. All these things are unavoidable. I looked less tidy than before, but I never slept in the street, I shaved every day, and if I lost weight it was because I wasn't hungry. When it was time I went home to sleep, but you can't stay there all day, from the hall to the living room and back to my room again, I didn't set foot in my mother's bedroom and didn't make the kitchen dirty or the flat as a whole, and the same goes for the bathroom, which I have never liked using.

I couldn't stay there. You can't stay in the flat all day long. You stand at the window and your breath makes it steam up and then it starts to run down the pane. No one can just walk around all day, on Sundays you go for a walk, on weekdays you go shopping or perform some other errand, and if neither of these things applies and you're wandering about in the city you inevitably go downhill, you deteriorate. However careful you are your clothes get dirty, and anyone sitting on benches for too long will end up with sores on his legs in winter; other people can tell at once when somebody doesn't know where to go, after all everyone must know where they're going, a person must know where he belongs.

I've spent my whole life protecting people, and suddenly there I was, wandering around the city in a thick winter coat not knowing where to go or when the day would at last come to an end, and anyone could point a finger at me and ask what business I had to be there, as if I were one of those madmen or cripples, one of those whom anybody has the right to ask what business he has to be there, and I for my part didn't have an answer. I've never been much of a talker, but when people asked me for information I was able to give it, and if anybody put himself in danger or was endangering other people I called out loudly enough for everyone to hear what I was saying. That time is over. Like an animal you creep away and hide, you're afraid of the looks you get from passers-by; time lingers like guilt.

It wasn't well built. I know now that it was downright shoddy. The walls are not real walls, they are made of mortar, iron struts and straw, and the straw is rotting, the iron rusting, the mortar breaking out of the wall and crumbling to dust.

It was my responsibility to keep an eye on the others so that nothing would happen to them. Now the others were watching me, looking at me with suspicion or with indifference—a dirty coat, the tired way of walking—, when somebody has nothing to do and doesn't know where to go, it shows, it's as if you had lost your face, as if you had a bad rash and still wanted to go into the water. Others are put off, even disgusted by the sight of you. A person like that has no business to be in the Swimming Baths. People steer clear of you, act as if you weren't there, and if you're sitting on a bench no one sits down next to you, as though you had the plague or had sneaked into the baths with running sores, with skin rashes or without having washed, which is strictly prohibited. It was up to me to ensure that those rules were observed.

You sit quite still and wait, ignoring the cold and the dirt. Whether it is your fault or not makes no difference. They can't imprison me in a flat. I walked along the passage and in the mornings I'd go and stand at the window waiting for it to get light. In the winter it takes a long time, you're afraid that it will remain dark, and as the dawn begins to appear you're already starting to wait for the evening, for it to be time, at last, to sleep, though you can't sleep and you lie awake waiting for first light, you can only see the windows and you know very well that tomorrow, too, you'll see nothing but the walls of some buildings and a bit of sky and a bit of street, the heads of passers-by, the roofs of cars, until in the end you feel like running down there and asking anyone who happens to be passing what your own name is because you have almost forgotten it yourself. Even the dead have names, I thought, and then remembered with a jolt that my mother's ashes were in an unnamed urn.

The shops were shut, the streets empty, I had forgotten that it was December, Christmas. I never liked Christmas any-way, I had to stay at home on those days because the Swimming Baths were closed, and although I saw the colored lights I'd take no notice of them. A very long time ago, while my father was still alive, we used to celebrate Christmas, but afterwards we didn't. About fifteen years ago, the year when I got to know Cremer and his daughter, I went out on Christmas Day because they had invited me round. I had bought a teddy bear for Tanja. Three years later Tanja was dead, and Cremer closed the kiosk for a whole week as if he had gone away on holiday. Now that I don't see Cremer any more no one uses my name.

"Guten Morgen, Hugo. Good morning." Cremer used to say every morning, calling me Hugo because that was what Tanja called me.

I would go and see Cremer, I thought on the third day, the kiosk would surely be open, I would go out but only as far as Cremer's kiosk, I wouldn't walk around all day, my outdoor shoes were ruined, the right sole was coming off, the heels were worn down, I must get them mended, I thought, Cremer would help me. You want to do something, anything, but know that it's no use. I wasn't going to go back to wandering the streets for whole days at a time, no one can expect that of me, nor that I should stay in the flat; I was never off sick. I would go and see Cremer, I thought, and went to comb my hair, and when I saw my face I thought: Not even Cremer would recognize me.

For my supper I used to eat whatever my mother had cooked at lunchtime. There'd be a saucepan on the stove and I would heat up the food before I went to bed, and if she hadn't cooked anything I would have some bread and cheese, and every morning I collected my two rolls from Cremer and ate them in the baths at midday, if possible in the small corner of the men's changing room which was partitioned off for the lifeguard's use and where I left my clothes during the day, for one shouldn't eat anything by the pool in case crumbs fell into the water. The bathers were strictly forbidden to bring any food in with them.

I didn't want to look at that face in the mirror. There's a mirror fixed to the wall of the passage between the entrance hall and the pool area, I passed it every day and noticed that I was getting older, but I hadn't changed very much, a narrow face and strongly-defined eyebrows, as dark as my hair, and if I looked serious that was all to the good, for the bathers were supposed to obey my instructions. I never thought much about my face, and although I was never very powerfully built no one was in any doubt that I was the lifeguard.

After my father's death my mother made some pink curtains, bought a pink bath mat, there was hardly room to move between the basin and the bath, and everything you touched was pink and smelled of eau-de-Cologne.

I was about to comb my hair before going to see Cremer, but the face in the mirror was thin and pale. I had got thinner. When I first met Cremer and said I was the lifeguard, he laughed.

He won't recognize me, I thought. One can't go around looking like this. The sharply-etched lines, as if the face had been scratched all over and were falling apart, eyes like hollow caverns, and I hadn't had a haircut for a long time, my hair was shaggy and hung down over my forehead, I couldn't go to any barber's looking like that, or to see Cremer, I wished I could wash that face off, but there isn't enough water to do that, I thought. Do you hear me? I didn't want to stand there any longer.

I left the flat. I didn't lock the door but just closed it behind me, didn't turn on the light on the stairs, and because the soles were coming off my shoes I was wearing my trainers as I used to, and my footsteps were completely silent. I know by heart what it says on the notices in the Swimming Baths:

People with broken skin or rashes are not allowed to use the pool.

I made a big detour before finally arriving at the Baths. The stone figures on the façade are badly weathered and have been so for a long time, for as long as I have known them, but I never paid any attention to them because I always went straight up the entrance steps and into the building. Now I was standing in front of it for the second time since my dismissal, I saw the piece of white cardboard attached to the door and read what was written on it. I saw the big padlock, a chain, the front windows boarded up, with everything dead behind them.

Two of the stone figures had been knocked off, two of the eight water nymphs supporting a basin in which Neptune sits. Above the portal, the bear being washed by two round-cheeked children was still there, but inside, on the other side of the door, there was nothing but dirt and emptiness.

I never made my voice heard. I should have called out so loudly that everything stopped, that time turned back, that the pool was never empty, that the water had never been drained off, then I would have been able to come here every day and be the lifeguard as before.

I have never committed an unlawful act. I had left the flat, didn't know where to go, had no plan or purpose in mind when I stood in front of the People's Baths, it was starting to get light, for a moment I thought it was all a mistake, I went up the steps as though I need only open up and go in through the entrance door and everything would be just as it had always been.

I was afraid that someone might recognize me, or that Cremer might come by and not recognize me. It would very soon be daylight, another day. I'm not a homeless person, I thought.

The padlock chain was rusty, as though it was not worth getting a new chain for such a dilapidated building. I looked around: apart from me the street was deserted. Just as I was about to go away I suddenly remembered my globe, which I had given to Klaus to keep for me. The globe might still be there, I thought, in the basement, and without stopping to think I went through the vehicle entrance into the yard, took the key out of my pocket as though I had remembered all along that I had the key to the side door, opened it and found myself facing the stairs down to the boiler room.

Chapter five

Someone might have been looking out of a window and seen me go through the vehicle entrance to the yard, unlock the side door; they might have seen me disappear inside, while at the main entrance, plain for all to see, a notice stating: *The swimming pool is closed, the People's Baths are closed.* Perhaps someone was suspicious and knocked on the main door; I have an idea that I heard knocking, two or three times, but the Baths are closed and I didn't answer.

I know that my entry here was unauthorized, but I didn't break in. I had the key. No one had told me to hand in the key to the side entrance. I pulled the door to behind me, stood facing the stairs leading down to the boiler room, couldn't turn the light on, it was dark. The smell boded no good. I groped my way forward in the dark, not daring to switch on the light in case someone notice that the building wasn't empty; I had got here at last. The door clicked shut behind me.

The smell came from the boiler room, and for a moment I felt like turning round and going away again, I would have gone away and perhaps never come back, but I was afraid of being seen by somebody outside. I stayed there all day, went as far as the passage, a few times up as far as the door, it had grown light by then, I wanted to wait until it got dark. The narrow windows of milky glass in the basement which are supposed to let in light from the yard were so dirty that I could hardly make out anything at all, and I didn't dare switch on the light. Only in the small windowless washroom did I finally put a light on, and I washed my hands and drank a little water from the tap. I sat down on a chair in the boiler room, not daring to go up straight away, I wanted to go up to the pool hall but stayed sitting down below for a long time, until I could bear the cold and the foul smell no longer, and quietly, as though someone might hear me, went up the stairs.

Now I know everything. No one need go looking for me, there are microphones, after all, every word that I say up here by the pool can be recorded, and my presence here can be established without anyone needing to come specially to the baths. But I didn't break in. The caretaker himself issued me with the key, I have not committed a punishable offence. I can explain everything.

I believed that I had to come back here.

For almost five weeks I had wandered around blindly, with the key in my pocket. I never wanted to be here. When I caught a whiff of the stench, when I had closed the door behind me, I realized that it was use. There was no other place where I could possibly stay.

The stench was dreadful, and in the dark it would have been easy to trip and fall on the stairs. No one must find me, I thought, nobody would find me here. I didn't know what was causing the stench, and in my mind it became mingled with the smell of hair spray, eau-de-Cologne and chlorine. It was a stench of decay, putrid and so pungent that it made my eyes water. Now there's a smell of dust, of coal dust. But I still have that other smell in my nostrils, when I wake up in the night, too, and even during the day, even up here, and then it seems to me as if the dead bodies are lying there before my eyes. Without the light from the globes I can't get to sleep. I haven't slept for nights on end. It's because of the images in my mind, I don't know how they got there, perhaps someone else saw them, or it's the water, it's what you see when for years all you've had before your eyes is water and naked bodies. Human beings are ugly. If their naked bodies don't lie it's only because they can't do it convincingly, because they betray themselves, their envy and their malice, all the cunning, the tedious ugliness which very quickly surrenders any little bit of pride or charm they may have had. In the Swimming Baths there is no disguise. I know what I'm talking about, and when Frau Karpfe informed me that I was dismissed I ought to have been glad that it was over. Pity and hatred, every bruise, the slow movements of a woman looking at herself in a mirror and seeing her age, the defiance with which she puts on a bright floral swimming costume; the turn of a young girl's head as she gets out of the water watched by a boyfriend, licking drops of water from her shoulder; babies crawling about naked on the tiles in the warm atmosphere. Nakedness, and the emptiness it leaves behind.

Day in, day out the bathers, the old people in the morning, in the afternoons the children and towards evening the others, a man washing himself, and his wife using her varnished fingernails to pull a tiny hair from her nipple; swollen feet, the soft flesh. I have seen it all and not said a word.

The People's Baths have been in existence for almost a hundred years. Anyone who was here in those days is long dead, and it seems to me as if the dead were returning, like me, as if

I were imprisoned here with them. Like shadows they sit in the gallery, waiting to see what will happen.

I don't know how they come to be here. They didn't die here. But I have a distinct sense that there is someone up in the gallery, and the others left long ago, I haven't seen any of them recently—neither the caretaker nor Frau Karpfe nor Klaus— and yet I'm well aware that there's someone in the pool hall, up in the gallery, and sometimes in the pool too.

I was the lifeguard here, for decades, I can definitely tell whether there's someone here or not. I am not duped by the microphones, nor by the fact that someone can hear what I'm saying, can demand that I explain what right I had to come in here. The others are certainly present, even if one can't hear them. I don't know what they want of me. Here no one has rights any more. All of this is just because of the water, that's the only reason they are here, just like me, and they brush against me with their shadowy arms, flit past me or stand, rigid and reproachful, at the side of the pool, as if I had done them some wrong.

I thought that the foul smell came from the pool. I immediately remembered what the old lifeguard told me, about dead bodies lying stretched out on the tiles, left to rot so that no one should be able to tell how they died.

I stood there for a long time, in the darkness, on the stairs, they also form a narrow passage like the passage linking the boiler room and the pool area, just wide enough for one person. You feel the walls close to your body, the paint is flaking, and with it a layer of soot, which has settled there over the years, it's a passage that hardly anyone uses except the boiler man. But it's far easier for the boiler man to reach the boiler room by coming across the yard, since the basement is only half underground, milky glass panes let in some light, and just a few steps lead down to a heavy iron door.

No one liked using the side entrance.

You find yourself in something resembling a tunnel between two internal doors, one leading back to the side entrance via a small anteroom, the other, made of iron, leading into the boiler room. The old lifeguard said that people were once held captive there. It's a narrow passage, I can barely avoid bumping my head on the ceiling, and the walls to left and right almost touch my body. Where someone has passed through, no trace of him remains, and anyone who was imprisoned here has disappeared leaving no sign, just like a person getting up and walking away, like the old lifeguard, and like me.

In the pool area it's different because here there was the water and, in the water, the naked bodies and what detaches itself from them, like a thin residue or a smell: not everything has wholly disappeared, and when I see the pool I know exactly who has been in it. Sometimes I dream that I have got stuck in the passage, or that the walls have closed in and I'm imprisoned between them. I don't like going along the passage. I've used it a few times because there was no other way for me to get out of the building, but when I think of it now it seems an impossibility for me ever to go along it again.

Up here there was the water, day after day, staring me right in the face.

The old lifeguard maintained that after the war there were corpses lying in the empty pool, that they were shot in the People's Baths and Swimming Pool.

Don't you know that he's an informer? Klaus whispered, pointing to the caretaker. Do you suppose they haven't been watching all of you? I always took care not to hear anything. If someone records what I say it's all the same to me, I'm not worried about that. Now I want to be listened to. Now I want them to hear that nothing happened in the Baths in all the years, all those years, no one drowned, a whole lifetime, day after day, as if the days were an account that had to be paid, without one's knowing why, without knowing how it was incurred or by what measure it is assessed. The measure is a ruined life, the water is the measure, the water in the early morning, the first light on the surface of the water, the quietness in the evening after the last few people have left the baths, the bodies and how unremarkable they are, the lion heads just below the gallery, on the pillars the painted flowers; the comings and goings of the bathers, the faces of the swimmers, their swimming up and down, the looks, movements, the growing older, and the memory of all the years—for almost a hundred years the People's Baths have been here, countless voices, the fear, the dead bodies on the floor of the pool, the indifference of the walls which are now decaying.

It should not have come to an end. That was the one thing about it: that it had no end, like water itself. No beginning and no end.

Traces can be falsified, and where there is a history, a different story can be told. In the water there are no traces, no impression and no sign, only naked bodies, as though one left everything in the water, as though one could wash the traces off one's skin, and everything would remain here.

From the outside no one can tell that I have come in here. I'm regarded as a missing person. The flat is sealed up. I had no plan, I had been sent packing, dismissed. You think that if you do nothing wrong everything will turn out well in the end, but that isn't true. And, after all, I only used the key that was given to me. How else could I have got in here? The main entrance is not only locked but also secured by a chain, the doors leading in to the boiler room from the yard are made of iron, well maintained and repainted every year, the caretaker attached great importance to preventing anyone from breaking in. There may be some people who think that a lifeguard and a caretaker are the same thing. After all, what does a lifeguard have to do, since it's very rare for anyone to drown in the Baths? And if the lifeguard has nothing to do, then he can easily take on the duties of a caretaker as well, duties which are also rather nebulous, since after all there is a technician, and plumbing jobs are done by the plumber, and if there is both a lifeguard and a caretaker then the one has nothing to do but dust the life-belt, while the other changes a light bulb every so often. People think the lifeguard and the caretaker are both lazy, so that it would be easy to manage without one of them. But that's not true. Precisely because nothing has happened, people forget that that is the lifeguard's doing. I did everything that could be expected of me, and it's unjust for the caretaker to be given a new job and the lifeguard not.

If I hadn't come back, there might have been a disaster, you get it? The foul smell was a bad omen. Even I almost ran away from it. It's a narrow passage, you don't know what there might be at the end of it. I groped my way slowly forward, unable to see anything, and the smell got worse. Then I opened the door to the boiler room.

There are four rooms in the basement: the big one containing the three boilers, with a door leading out into the yard, a coal store, a third room with a big table and tools, and then the small room with the cupboard and the plank bed.

In the boiler room there is another table where Klaus used to sit and eat, and he cooked in the tool room where the big pipes lead to safety valves, which release hot steam when you open them. Then the pipes continue up to the floor above.

When I took the globe to Klaus, both of the aquariums were standing in the tool room. He had two aquariums, one with small fish, and the other with big fish, for which he scooped water out of the swimming pool.

"Not carp," he said, grinning, "more's the pity!" Then he took the globe from me and stood it next to the fish.

Several weeks had passed since the baths were closed. I don't know anything about fish, and I can't think why Klaus left them here, because if they're not fed they'll inevitably die of starvation. He couldn't have anticipated that I would come back—the whole building is closed, nobody is allowed to be in here, and up in the entrance hall there's a notice:

Achtung! Caution! Danger of collapse!

For the fish it meant certain death.

I didn't notice the aquarium at once, the panes of milky glass are so grimy that they barely let any light in. I didn't know what it was that was rotting away here, it was a smell of decay, the boilers were cold, and then on the table I discovered the bigger aquarium, in which four fish were slowly swimming about, the fifth was floating on the surface of the turbid water, and later I saw that it was half eaten. In the tool room the stench was even worse, the second aquarium was a black box, you couldn't see anything in it; on the floor nearby, in the dirt, was a silvery fish, dusty and shriveled up.

I picked it up, placed it carefully in the palm of my hand, it seemed fragile, being so dry; carrying it on the flat of my hand I took it up the stairs to the pool area, as though there it would be sure to recover.

It was weightless, it's odd to carry something in your hand and not feel it at all, and my steps, too, were light, and everything would be all right again now; I went upstairs as if this were what I was intended to do, as if it were an action as familiar to me as the pool had been, I advanced straight to the edge, walked along the very edge of the pool to the steps by which the non-swimmers used to enter the shallow water, carefully went down them and on to where the water gets deeper, and laid the dead fish gently down on the turquoise tiles.

It's still lying there.

Yes, it's lying there still, perhaps in time it will shrivel or finally be reduced to dust; I don't know what happens to dead bodies if they just lie there like that. Cremer's daughter Tanja was driven away in the ambulance, I didn't see her again after that, but sometimes I imagine her lying here at the baths, quite still, completely dried out and very light, just as she really was light when I carried her in my arms because Cremer's hands were shaking. She wouldn't like to see the swimming pool like this, because she enjoyed swimming, though just for a short time she might have found it fun to have the whole building to herself.

But that's neither here nor there, and the thought of the dust would be still more unbearable if she were lying there, a dead child, in the dust. She would have grown up long ago, there's no point in thinking about it, only the thought does sometimes cross my mind when I see the empty pool with the dead fish lying in it, nothing but a tiny patch.

When I think of my parents and of Tanja, it seems to me that not all dead people are dead in the same way, even if most of them come to terms with their new condition, and ultimately there's no reason to miss them. You think of them in the same way as you think of the time of day or anything else that is inescapable.

Perhaps I too might have got used to the present state of affairs and seen it as the only possible one, if another slab of plaster and paint had not broken away from the wall and landed on the floor with a barely perceptible noise. Now I wait. It may happen again at any time. As soon as I stop speaking, the silence becomes unbearable, all that remains is the expectation that yet another slab will break away from the wall.

The night before last a paw broke off one of the stone lions. Now the leg that pokes out below the face is too short. The stone just crumbled away. The baths are decaying, one day they'll be demolished without anyone saying a word.

I had come back and was standing at the edge of the

pool, looking up at the clock—this was before it stopped—and watching the second hand moving round. I said nothing; it was very quiet. If only I were back at the baths, I had thought, as if that would be a deliverance, as if then everything would fall into place again. The hands of the clock were moving, and even if I looked away I could still hear them. Apart from that it was quiet, only time was left, and it passed so slowly that I stood there motionless and didn't know what I could do.

When the slab, about half a yard across, broke away from the wall and the hole was deeper than the first time, so deep that rusting struts were exposed, when I heard that noise, followed by the silence, it made me think of my first day back here. I can't say exactly how long I've been here now, but it must be some weeks.

From the basement I fetched a broom and a metal bucket. I removed the loose dirt as well as I could, but the dust is everywhere and I wasn't very successful. I did my best, sweeping all round the pool carefully so as not to stir up the dust.

Then I saw the notices, and the writing on them, and realized that they no longer mean a thing.

It's like in winter when it snows in the night, when you see the smooth white roadway and are suddenly afraid that it's forever, that no one will ever come.

I am not going to open the door to anyone. At times it seems to me that someone is knocking, someone from outside who either wants to come in or is just doing it for a joke, perhaps a child, perhaps an angry bather; then I stand quite still and most of the time it's probably just a mistake, a knocking in the heating system, a rustling, but I'm going to take precautions to ensure that no one can get in—I wouldn't want anyone to come in—I'll put a padlock on the inside of the main door, and at the side entrance I'll leave the key in the lock so that the door can't be unlocked from the outside.

I know that there's nothing I could do if a decision were taken to force the doors, just as I can't prevent the building from being demolished, but until that happens no one is going to get in here.

Before the second slab broke out of the wall I hadn't considered the possibility that someone might be able to hear me. I wasn't saying anything. My father had drummed it into me that you don't talk to yourself. According to him I wasn't normal. Is there anybody listening here?

Nothing left in the pool area, or on the stand, the lion heads mute, yellowish paint peeling from the wall, the handrails around the pool and on the stairs are going green, the flowers on the pillars are pale, and it's hard to imagine now that people once came here daily to swim, got undressed, leapt into the water; everything is so quiet that you can still hear footsteps, the soft padding of bare feet.

I took my shoes off, and my socks, walking barefoot around the pool, on the cold floor. There seemed to be others following me, a long line of them, in swimming trunks or in bathrobes or naked, the old ones naked, the dead ones, with me at their head.

The stench of decay that came from the boiler room spread along the passage into the pool area. It didn't vanish.

I can still smell it. Sometimes I think they're already waiting, they're sitting up in the gallery, they're leaning on the walls of the passage to the entrance hall, they're walking to and fro in the changing rooms, there are more and more of them, it's as if you were walking through a crowd of people and yet you can't hear a sound. I don't know if they're on my side. I shan't wait much longer now. It's enough; I haven't thought of a solution yet, but soon I shall find one.

Every day I saw how quickly bodies grow weary, and how hard it is for them to find rest.

You won't hear anything from me that can be used.

I haven't been outside for some days now. The flat is sealed up, and perhaps they're searching for me, perhaps they've put out a notice about my having gone missing and people are supposed to report any sighting of me. I'm not going out any more.

How long I stood there I don't know. The foul smell and the cold made me feel sick, and I was tired.

Frau Karpfe took one of the benches for herself. I haven't dared to go into the entrance hall, and up to now I have kept away from her office.

Finally I went back down to the basement. I was afraid of the stench. It was only the fish but I know nothing about fish. I didn't know what to do, I thought of going out, leaving everything as it was, the coldness and the empty pool, the single dead fish in it, the pool hall which had an eerie feel and might collapse and bury me under it. No one knew where I was, no one would come looking for me.

The tiles in the pool are gray, the water is missing, and when the tiles are exposed to the air and the cold, they contract until they crack away from the wall. I didn't want to hear it. So I went down into the basement.

I finally sorted out where things were: in front of the big boilers the table, on it the aquarium with the fish that were still alive, in the tool room the small fish that were dead. The big boilers, the coal store, a wheelbarrow, a shovel, all of it looking as if the boiler man had only just gone out and might be back at any moment, and only the smell proof that no one had been here for weeks.

On the surface of the water in the aquarium the dead fish floated, already half decayed, the water cloudy, scummy; putting my hand into it was nauseating, first I had to take the fish out, I looked for a container and found an empty jar, then I looked for a bag, couldn't find one, took a plastic beach bag from the lost property cupboard, and into put the five fish corpses and some gravel and plastic plants, rolled the bag up tightly and put it by the door to the passage that leads to the outside. Alongside the room with the plank bed and the cupboard is the small washroom, and I lugged the aquarium in there, meaning to empty the water out into the shower, but the aquarium was heavier than I thought, it slipped out of my hands and smashed.

The stinking water formed a puddle on the floor with shards and splinters of glass in it, and I cut myself on them. I didn't know how to stanch the flow of blood because the first aid box had been taken away, the blood dripped on to the floor and on to my jacket, which I hadn't taken off. So I had no choice but to put the light on, I searched in the small room and in the tool room, finally got some toilet paper and took a scarf from the lost property cupboard, I never set out to be a thief, there were towels and swimming things lying in a muddled heap, spattered with blood, my jacket and shirt were smeared with it, I took the jacket off; it was very cold. Once my hand was bandaged I quickly turned out the light because it might be seen from outside and no one must know that there's anybody in here. When you become a lifeguard you learn how to treat injuries and bandage an open wound. But there had never been any necessity for it because no accident had ever happened, and when the woman collapsed in the changing room that had nothing to do with the Baths.

I sat down on a chair in the boiler room. Then I went back upstairs.

I tore the plastic sheeting from the wall. Did you hear the sound that made? Because of the nails that I pulled out with it, the size of the hole increased; I took the plastic to the changing room, it's still lying there. In the tool room I found a shovel and a broom. I didn't manage to make much of a difference.

Sometimes I think that the bathers will surely be back any minute, the pool will be filled up again and everything will be back to normal. Then I see the walls, the yellowing paint, see that the tiles are coming loose, just as on that first day I found a loose tile under my feet as I walked in the pool, carefully detached it and later took it down to the basement, it lay on the table there in front of the aquarium, the fish almost motionless, only four of them still alive, perhaps they would have eaten each other up as they had eaten the dead fifth fish and the sixth fish, which was why they hadn't died of starvation. They were swimming slowly to and fro, just as I had always walked to and fro beside the pool. I ought to stick the tile back, I had thought, change the water in the aquarium; I didn't know how one is supposed to catch the fish, I didn't dare to touch them.

I thought I would leave as soon as it was dark, but with my injured hand wrapped in the bloodstained scarf, going out into the street seemed too risky. I needed to buy adhesive for the tile, and fish food, and I hadn't eaten anything but only drunk water from the tap in the washroom. I was afraid that it would be obvious where I had come from and that I'd be arrested. I looked for a blanket because I felt cold, couldn't find one and ended up taking two towels, I couldn't stand the smell in the basement, so I went up into the pool hall again, there I sat down on the bench and perhaps I did fall asleep, with the towels draped around my shoulders and over my stomach.

All night long it was dark, because I didn't dare turn the light on. A feeble glimmer of light came into the pool area from the street. I had brought the tile back upstairs with me and placed it next to me on the bench, the towels had a musty smell, they were fraying at the edges and first fluff and then whole bits of material stuck to my uninjured hand. These benches force you to sit bolt upright, Frau Karpfe had taken the other one for her garden.

"Do you want the life-belt as a souvenir?" the caretaker had asked, grinning. But that doesn't matter any more, the life-belt can't save anybody now.

I sat there all night like someone keeping vigil by a dead body. In the dark the pool area seemed much bigger, it seemed to be expanding, but that's an illusion. I could hear a soft grinding noise, a grinding of teeth, and I sat there as if I were keeping vigil by a dead body, I couldn't leave without arousing the anger of the dead. You sit bolt upright, not knowing if you're waiting or keeping watch, perhaps one person isn't enough, but there's no one here apart from me, they all left without a word of protest.

I wanted to get away. All night long I was wishing I could leave at last. I sat on the bench under the gallery, under the lion faces, a feeble glimmer of light coming in through the glass bricks opposite, the pool area seemed too vast for me to cross, I would never be able to reach the steps to the basement by morning, somewhere on the way I would perish, and in the pool, in the darkness, I thought I could see people swimming in the empty pool, patiently doing their lengths and looking spitefully up at me.

I'm not going out into the street any more. Early retirement or unemployed, it's all the same, I've seen those others, they wander the streets or stand about, drunk, they sit at bus stops, and you see them in the supermarkets, most of them are very quiet and polite, they're in no hurry, they have all the time in the world, shoulders hunched so as to take up less room, faces even grayer than usual in winter, the gray is etched into their skin and their eyes, every movement is cautious, as though they might break something, and only their hands tremble as they count out the money.

I sat there all night. Thought I saw swimmers; Cremer's daughter was there too, she was wearing a bathing cap over her light-colored hair, her face bare and narrower than before, her limbs thin, I was concerned that she wouldn't be able to swim, but I couldn't move, couldn't call out to her, I didn't know her name, I did know that she hadn't long to live, but perhaps it was a different child, I thought she was going to be killed, and I saw my father, he seized her by the arm as if she were standing at the edge of the pool and had to go down into it, about to be pushed down into it, my father looked very calm, then he seemed to roar out something, perhaps a command, there were many children, women, they were all wearing bathing caps, among them Cremer's daughter, whom I couldn't recognize, they had bald pates, as ugly as dead people, then the sound of footsteps, regular and loud, I was afraid they were coming, they'd found me, the caretaker was standing next to a man I didn't know, pulling him towards the side entrance, giving him the key, then it was Klaus feeding his fish with torn-up documents, and now the fish have grown, they're getting bigger and bigger, I knew nothing about it, saw my mother reading letters and then she burned the letters, burned photos, she too was in uniform, then she cut my hair short, I wanted to leave, I wanted to say, it's time to go, but there was no time and the distance was too great, the old lifeguard made a weary gesture, he unlocked the doors, saw what was in the pool and vomited, later he pulled two men over to the narrow passage between the side entrance and the boiler room, he was trying to explain something but they weren't listening, it was very dark.

It was cold, the towels provided no warmth, they smelled musty as though the damp had been trapped in them, there was fluff sticking to my hand, pink like my mother's curlers, I wanted to say that I'd been mistaken for someone else, it's the old lifeguard who's here, not me. Then I remembered Tanja's name, the other bathers came one after another, they were transparent like X-ray images, and suddenly as I looked at each one I thought

I knew something of his or her life. I had never made that my business, so long as they didn't drown their life was no concern of mine; I didn't want to know anything about them, whether one of them was desperate, another one happy, they sometimes wore bathing caps and then their faces were rigid, I saw it, the naked bodies and the water, I smelled the odor, the chlorine can't disguise it, the cleanliness of the water is an illusion, everything stays in the water, invisible particles which are now stuck to the tiles in the pool. The dead fish was lying in the pool, I didn't want to stay here any longer, but in the early morning light the pool was full of water, heavy, murky water like the water from the aquarium with the dead fish, I feared that at any moment it would drain away, and I wanted to call for help, it mustn't happen, this pool mustn't be empty again. And the building was breaking up into its component parts, huge cracks, the tiles fracture in the cold, it won't even be necessary to demolish it.

In the morning I woke up confused, my arms and legs awkward. Everything sticks in your mind, you'd like to put your hand into your mind and feel around to see what's in there, just as you do with the big filter which catches hairs and fluff and everything else that falls into the water and doesn't immediately sink to the bottom, you have to check the filter every day so that it doesn't get clogged up, it's the flocculent that binds things together into clumps made up of minute particles, your fingers don't know what it is they're touching; I used to check the filter every morning, the strainer in it is sensitive, and if you don't keep an eye on the quality of the water there can easily be a disaster—if you don't spot immediately that the water has reached its pollution threshold. The fluctuations of the water quality are very subtle and you have to weigh up carefully what needs doing. They would make fun of me, the caretaker and Frau Karpfe, but if the water passes that threshold you have to let it out and close the pool.

On that morning the water was cloudy. I had fallen asleep on the wooden bench, the cold and the stink woke me up. You shouldn't sleep in the street, the cold opens up sores on your legs, they take you away, it's immediately obvious when a person is down and out, you can tell by their shoes. I couldn't bear the dirt, the smell, I stood up and got undressed, thinking that I would have a swim, after all there was no one there, I thought I would go into the water as I was, just this once, without taking a shower first, because there was no water in the changing rooms. I would wash off all these days and weeks, then the error would be rectified. I hadn't swum for a long time, the lifeguard doesn't have to swim, but perhaps that was the mistake.

My arms and legs were numb and awkward, the towels had not warmed me, I folded them, took off my shoes, jacket, shirt and trousers, for a moment I felt embarrassed because I had no swimming trunks with me, then I undressed completely and went down the shallow steps at the non-swimmers' end.

It was very cold. At the other end of the pool, where the pool is three meters deep, I was startled because the water is too deep for you to be able to stand there.

Twenty-five meters from one end of the pool to the other, going lengthways, the gray-green tiles were ice-cold, dusty, and then three meters deep, I went into a corner, not wanting anyone to see me naked, I was shivering with cold, I needed to get back to the bench where my clothes were lying, twenty-five meters. I kept so close to the edge that my arms brushed against the tiles, the rail above me, then alongside me, my head above water again, the cold, my bare feet, no water, only the dust.

In the dust on the tiles you can make out the shape of a body, there's no dust there, it shows up when the sun shines, the shape of a body lying there, not moving.

Then I woke up.

How much time I had missed I can't say, hours or days.

If an hour can be missing as though it had never been, then you can't feel certain of anything any more. Finally I stood up, picked up my clothes, went down to the basement, still undressed, saw the aquarium with the catfish, the water smelled foul, I found the jar and kept scooping filthy water out until the fish were almost lying on the bottom and desperately gulping for air. Four black fish, they lay there thrashing about, I thought they were dying and waited, but it takes a long time; I would wait, I thought, and once they were dead I could go.

But the fish were tough and refused to die, my injured hand was painful, I picked up my clothes, stood, still naked, in front of the aquarium; coal dust, ashes on the floor, the boilers idle, cold, touched the big boilers with my uninjured hand, I'd go out, I thought, and didn't know where. I wished the fish would hurry up and die, but they thrashed about, gulping for air as if they were drowning, time passes very slowly when you're waiting. They won't open the baths again. It doesn't matter, and everything has been arranged, early retirement, the others gone, they have jobs or they're unemployed, no one will come here any more.

I understand that now, do you hear me?

No one will come.

I stood there motionless, watching the fish which wouldn't stop thrashing about, wouldn't stop living. Finally I fetched some fresh water, filled up the aquarium, had a wash at the washbasin and put my clothes on.

Chapter six

I took the key, unlocked the door from the inside, and locked it behind me. There could be no question of my having broken in. I left the Swimming Baths of my own free will. Only when I was on my way to the flat did I remember the globe. I had forgotten it, and I ought to feed the fish, I thought, feeling uneasy, although I had carefully locked the door.

I had gone back because of the globe, and had forgotten the globe because of the fish. No one would feed the fish, they would eat each other one by one until the last one died of starvation, in the end one fish would remain and would die of starvation, I thought, and I made a detour to avoid Cremer's kiosk. I didn't want anyone to see me, and I managed to get into the flat unobserved.

No one was waiting for me there. I took off my shoes by the front door and went into the bathroom, washed my hands, particularly rinsing my injured hand, then I went into my room and sat down on the bed. I thought that I should change my clothes, have a shower, that I couldn't stay there, and I went into the kitchen, made some tea. In the kitchen cupboard there was a packet of crispbread—I've never liked using the bath-room—I wasn't hungry, the clock in the kitchen said ten o'clock, time didn't pass and later on it was still only half past ten.

I can explain everything.

Suddenly everything was easy. Taking my identity card and some money, I went out and bought everything I needed, tinned food, crispbread and fish food, I can show you my sup-plies, and packed some clothes and a blanket into a bag. I had something to eat before leaving the flat, I've never needed much. In the evening I went back to the baths with the bag over my shoulder, it was raining, hardly anyone was about, and when I turned into the yard and opened the side door no one called out. I was quite calm, I turned the key twice, quickly went through the narrow passage, the bag brushing against the walls, I carried it into the small room and at once set about lighting one of the boilers. The coal wouldn't catch alight to begin with, but in the end I had it burning brightly. I closed the boiler door, the hand that I'd cut on the bits of glass was hurting, it's still hurting now, there's a red scar running across the back of my hand, I had a temperature but it was all the same to me, I fed the fish and went to the lost property cupboard, hunted for my globe and found it tucked away in a corner right at the bottom. I was still afraid of being discovered here, since I'd reluctantly had the light on while I stoked the boiler. Now I turned it off, switched on the globe, went into the small room where the bed is, wrapped myself up in the blanket, got up again every so often to stoke the boiler. I must have fallen asleep, but when I woke up it was warm, and since I've been here the pool area has been heated, as it should be.

During the next few days I regularly returned to the flat, leaving the baths and entering the flat under cover of darkness, making detours to avoid Cremer's kiosk, and when I had shopping to do I took care not to go to places where I might be recognized. Previously I had very seldom done any shopping, except that I sometimes bought milk and packet soups for my mother from the small shop that had formerly stocked maps and travel books. At one time I often used to stand looking at the maps and globes and the books in the window, and although they stopped selling the travel guides after Unification I still liked to go there, they stayed open until late at night and sold long life milk and packet soups, tinned foods, cigarettes, alcohol and newspapers. For a time you could also take shoes there for mending, and usually until closing time there would be a few men standing at a tall round table drinking coffee or beer. Cremer was annoyed because the shop also sold newspapers and filled rolls, and it isn't far from his kiosk.

Only a few months ago they'd recognized me. Five men had looked up when I came in, two were in boiler suits, and the third had a belt around his waist with tools hanging from it.

"He's out of work!" the fourth one called across when he saw me looking at the tools, "But he's used to carrying the extra weight."

I didn't know them, I didn't know why they asked me to join them, the fifth one held out a can of beer to me, he was small and thin, his face a mass of brittle-looking lines which reached right up to his bald pate and almost made his steeply sloping nose disappear, and I didn't know him either.

Sometimes there was a table outside with a Perspex cover under which old magazines were displayed, or it might be slippers, gloves or socks, once there were corkscrews and kitchen knives, with a few maps in among them.

"Aren't you the lifeguard?" asked the woman who owned the shop, surprised, and the five men looked at me.

"Bit puny, isn't he?" said one of them.

"Not at the open-air pool," she explained, "the lifeguard from the People's Baths."

People aren't supposed to eat in the Swimming Baths, not in the changing rooms and certainly not near the pool, because whatever they might eat there would drip or crumble, there would always be some tiny scraps that would soften in the water and disintegrate. Any dirt sticks to bare feet and comes off in the water, where people flail about with their arms and legs, and then it sinks to the bottom and doesn't rise to the surface again, you don't even see streaks of dirt, but they are there, you know that, and they pollute the water.

Eating at the Swimming Baths is prohibited, and as long as you want to stay in the Baths you have to go hungry, either starve or leave, because only the lifeguard has a small room set aside for him, where I used to make a quick lunch of the two rolls from Cremer's kiosk.

Sometimes you see someone swimming with his mouth open, dribbling saliva out of the corners of his mouth, the way little children dribble milk or chocolate drinks down their chin. You can't say anything, and there's no telling whether a person is peeing in the water. You see the bodies, liver spots, warts, athlete's foot and yellow toenails, the skin with rolls of fat. It would certainly put you off your food, and no one is allowed to eat here. I have obeyed that rule, do you hear me? The food that I've brought in here is down in the boiler room, and as soon as I've finished eating I sweep the floor so that nothing gets picked up on the soles of my shoes. I always sweep up straight away, I sweep up after feeding the fish too, because the fish food is dry and flakes of it might fall outside the tank.

Even if I bring in things that have no business to be in a swimming bath I make sure that they stay in the basement, although the notices and rules have become pointless. Fish have no business to be in a swimming bath, not even in an empty and dusty pool. The dead fish is still lying there, the rules are futile now but I take great pains to obey them as far as possible.

There has never been a rule saying that one mustn't bring a globe in here. A globe does no harm. And given that two thirds of the earth's surface is water it would be appropriate to put up a globe in all Swimming Baths. Human beings are supposed to have come from the water, like all living creatures, and are said to consist mainly of water. There can't be any objection to it, and if the bottom of the pool is covered in dust that makes no difference, and even if the notices and warnings are pointless now because nobody comes here any more, because this place is an absurdity, a mistake, the borders on the globes have nothing to do with that.

My globe was in the bottom section of the lost property cupboard, it was in a dark corner and wasn't giving any light because it can't do that with the plug pulled out. You can't expect a model of the planet Earth to give light of its own accord as if its core were liquid, since what it has inside it is not a core but a light bulb. The bulb was still intact, as I found out when I retrieved the globe from the cupboard, stood it on the table, plugged it into a socket and pressed the switch. I wasn't surprised by this, I fully expected a globe to remain undamaged under all circumstances, and this is only now being proved wrong. For I didn't stop at one globe, I have three more globes here. One globe and a second one have already gone out, the third and fourth might start flickering at any time and ultimately go out too, and that's not my fault but the fault of circumstances.

The other three globes were ones that I found. Late one evening I was passing the shop which formerly sold maps and travel guides and which had now also closed down, where the owner had recognized me and was one of the bathers. There's no question of it being theft, and I was in the street because I was on my way to spend the night at the flat.

A lifeguard must not fall asleep in the Swimming Baths, I thought. Early each morning I returned there, hoping that the boilers wouldn't have gone out, since it's easier to get them going if they are still warm, and a building that isn't heated in winter will suffer irreparable damage. So I left the Baths late at night, although there was no boiler man, I wasn't just loitering about, I needed to buy something to eat and food for the fish, I hoped that in the dark no one would see me opening the side door and locking it behind me, and in spite of the boilers I slept at the flat, for a lifeguard who falls asleep can hardly be surprised if he's dismissed.

Now I stay in the basement with the fish and the globes. There are no rules down there, for fish have no more business to be in the Municipal Swimming Baths than does an empty pool that was once a swimming pool. When I found the three globes in a box at the shop, they were basically unsellable because the borders were now wrong. I hoisted the box, a big one, on to my shoulder and brought it here.

The borders are wrong, and whether something is the planet Earth or not makes no difference. The borders are wrong, just as the swimming pool is empty and there's dust where there used to be water. Brought the box with three globes in it here, it seemed a very long way although it took me no more than ten minutes, I was afraid I might be stopped, perhaps by the police, was afraid the globes might start shining, that everyone would immediately notice me, since in the dark a globe shines brightly, although its light is bluish because two thirds of the planet is covered by water.

It seemed a long way from the shop because the box was unwieldy and heavy, I had put it up on my shoulder and my shoulder hurt, in the past weeks and months I've grown thin, I've become a skinny-looking man whom no one would take on as a lifeguard, but nobody ever drowned, and I didn't drop the box; it was standing out in the street in front of the shop, nobody wanted it, those borders have had their day, and yet the light bulbs were still intact and after I found a four-way adaptor in the tool room they were all glowing without flickering.

The shutters were down, I had already noticed that as I passed by, they were grayish-black and dirty in front of the door, a little lighter alongside, where books and maps and atlases had once been displayed in the window. As a child I often stood there looking at them but later never went inside, since I had no use either for travel guides to our friendly neighbor states or for hiking maps, and when the borders weren't right any more they quickly stopped selling the maps, because maps and travel books are intolerant of incorrect names.

Now the shutters were closed for good, and I would have passed the shop without a second look if I hadn't seen the packing cases and a standard lamp outside, the tall table lying on its side on the pavement, the shutter on the door was only half down, and then I caught sight of a large cardboard box with an electric flex protruding from it.

If I hadn't chanced to find the box I would most probably have gone back to the flat to sleep, as on the preceding nights, but I wanted to take the globes to the Baths straight away, that same night.

Presumably, they had been kept for some time in the side room which once housed the shelves of books and later the boxes of tinned food, long life milk and packet soups and, in the winter, the round tables which were put outside in the summer. Either it was always the same men who went there to drink coffee and beer or sometimes schnapps, whether inside or outside, or they were different ones each time but resembled each other now that they were hanging around in the street, just loitering, whereas previously they had walked from one specific place to another, just as I had walked to and fro between the flat and the Baths.

"Perhaps we've come to resemble each other now that there are those others who look different," I said to Cremer a few months ago when he told me that among the men who now stood around outside the corner store, the shop that had formerly sold travel guides and maps, there were some who would once have bought rolls and a newspaper from him on their way to work. Instead of which, these people now spent hours standing at the round tables drinking coffee and beer, and also bought the paper there, and their rolls, and when I argued that there were always five of them and always the same ones, he gave an ill-tempered laugh.

Perhaps there is a resemblance between all those who walk along the street for no good reason, who loiter about in the street or in front of a shop because they're not required to be either at one specific place or another, and because they look alike it's uncertain exactly how many of them there are. It was the same a few years ago in the Swimming Baths when Frau Karpfe informed me that everyone now had to wear a bathing cap, and on the following day the caretaker put up a large notice in front of the corridor leading from the entrance hall to the pool area, saying that from now on nobody without a bathing cap would be admitted, and beneath those light-colored, hairless heads the faces were indistinguishable.

I was the lifeguard and said nothing. The writing on the notices that are here now is limited to a few instructions, which can't be misunderstood and can have no unforeseen consequences. I know that there were other notices, the caretaker found two of them behind a cupboard in one of the changing rooms: *Jews not welcome.*

Grinning, he stood them up in the entrance hall and left them there until the evening, when I put them away in the storeroom. In due course the caretaker hung the notice about the bathing caps in the pool hall itself.

The swimming pool isn't big, but the number of bathers was, and suddenly there seemed to be far more of them than usual because you couldn't tell the people in their bathing caps apart, every one of them in a bathing cap, the notice hung in the pool hall and no one was allowed into the water without a cap, as I constantly had to call out, pointing to the notice, the swimmers were not supposed to be in the pool area at all without a bathing cap, they already had smooth white skulls when they came out of the changing rooms. They would come wet, with white skulls, from the showers. Do you hear me? It's easy to make faces disappear, it doesn't take much for nothing at all to remain, and from there it's only a small step for them to be doing synchronized swimming, raising their heads, lowering them at the same time, as if on command.

They had no faces, they looked as if their heads had been shaved, and seemed obedient, and in the end I covered up the notice with a towel as though by doing that I could cover up those faces, which I found alien and ominous.

Perhaps this was where I slipped up, for I never looked at them, paying attention only to their bare bodies, their movements, and now they are returning, unrecognizable, hostile, as if there were some unfinished business between us.

That was the only rule that I broke. I observed the other rules just as the old lifeguard had instructed me to. There had never been a rule prohibiting toys from the pool area, and I took no action when a child brought in a toy, although I knew that it was not the done thing, for objects fall into the water, become saturated, sink to the bottom, and may possibly be dirty. Sometimes, a toy would be left behind and never collected, a plastic doll or a rag doll, a wooden animal, and no one came back to enquire about it. The same went for towels and swimsuits, and then I would pass whatever it was on to the boiler man, who would keep all the things in a cupboard in the basement. That does no harm.

If something is lost there's no need to worry, I thought, as I opened the cupboard in the basement which contained bathing caps, towels and a few toys; Klaus had moved the cupboard into his little room, and it was this cupboard that had my globe in it too.

I don't know what has become of the people who lost things, they've probably long since forgotten about it, they were children then and are grown up now, or they were grown up then and are now dead. And those who are still alive possibly wouldn't want the thing back that they once left behind. A piece of lost property which you get back isn't lost property any more. Perhaps it was a mistake to retrieve the old globe. Everything was quite safe in the cupboard. Even if the lost property is kept in the basement the lifeguard is ultimately responsible for it, and when Klaus wanted to throw away the accumulation of lost property I was able to stop him, so that something lost and found in the People's Baths was an object that would be safely preserved under all circumstances and for ever. Anything that has ever been here is still here.

If I hadn't chanced to find the other three globes in the street they would have been taken away by the dustmen the following morning, as my mother had intended my old globe to be taken away. I decided to bring the box with the three globes straight here, because the flat wouldn't be a safe place for them. So that night I came back here and slept in the small room where there's a folding camp bed; since then I've been spending the nights here.

It stays dark for a long time. Even now that the days are lengthening it still stays dark for a long time. I avoid putting the lights on in the pool hall, I never turn on more than the emergency lighting: someone might see the lights; an observant person can see them from outside. But the blue light of the globes won't betray me, and sometimes in the basement I pick up a globe and hold it like a lamp as I go from the tool room to the small room. If the flex were not so short I could carry it ahead of me when I go along the corridor. It would be the most appropriate light for this place now.

When the globes were standing on the table in front of the boilers, all four in a row, the whole boiler room was light enough to see, but now two of the globes have gone out. Last night a mouse scurried across the table, past the aquarium, in between the wooden bases of the globes, stood up on its hind legs and sniffed at one of the blue spheres. Then it ran on, stood up again, and it seemed to want to climb up on to the Earth, its paws reached Paraguay or Argentina, below them is Tierra del Fuego, the Land of Fire. The boilers are a good twelve feet tall, behind the mouse and the globes one of the boiler doors was open and I could see the flames, their reddish light, in front of that the blue light of the globes. Two of them have gone out, a third one is flickering. The mice are multiplying, and I've seen rats too.

If it were not for the flex one could carry a globe like a lamp, both hands around the wooden base that supports the metal arc holding the glass sphere, for the corridor leading to the pool is very dark at night, even in the daytime I can see almost nothing until I reach the stairs that go up to the pool area. It's only when you come to the foot of the stairs that you see a glimmer of light, before that it's as dark as if you were deep underground. So deep that no flight of stairs could ever provide a way out.

You no longer see anything at all.

People walk aimlessly to and fro as if they can no longer find the entrance. When the People's Baths were closed they said nothing, indeed some of them helped to bring it about—the walls, the pool not good enough, the water cloudy, the whole building antiquated. The caretaker showed himself more than willing to take them to Frau Karpfe's office so that they could address their complaints to her, so that Frau Karpfe could find reasons for not ordering more chlorine and flocculent, and when the inspectors came the water was not in perfect condition. This was exactly what they wanted; the others didn't say anything and neither did I. Now they're wandering through the corridors and the pool area in the dark, walking through the empty pool, there are more and more of them, and when I'm lying in the basement I can hear their footsteps, their breathing, and without the light of the globes it would be rather frightening.

I have rearranged the globes several times. If you want to prevent the coal dust from darkening the colors and the glass and eventually obscuring them completely, you have to clean the surface every day with either a dry or a damp cloth. I arranged the four globes first in a square, then in a row. Ultimately no decision is possible. A correct decision would have to be definitive, so that there could be no question in future of arranging the four globes differently. At first their place was on the table in the tool room, now they are standing in front of the boilers in the boiler room. The extension lead goes right across the tool room to the table, which also has the aquarium on it. Every day they need wiping, either with a dry or damp cloth, and perhaps that's what has caused the white points of light to appear, points which pierce the sea or a continent as if the interior of the Earth were infested with worms channeling their way to the surface.

Every day I wipe the globes and sometimes I carry them from the boiler room to the tool room or into the small room; then I bend down and put the extension lead where it needs to go. Perhaps the best place for the globes, two thirds of which consist of water, would be the pool. But in the water there'd be a short circuit and the globes would float like dead, blue-colored heads on the surface.

I spend a lot of time in the basement. From time to time I imagine that I'm the boiler man, either Klaus or a different boiler man, that I have nothing to do but shovel coal into the boiler fires and bring coal from the coal store into the main part of the basement. In the basement there's always something to do, and it's the warmest place. You can hear the fire in the boilers. There was never a coming and going of people here, it wasn't a place where several people would be present at any one time, except when the shifts changed, one man going, another coming to relieve him, because until Klaus was taken on there were always several of them, or at least there was a second boiler man. The fish belong to Klaus. If I were the boiler man, Klaus would have to come and relieve me. But he left the fish here. Even the catfish nearly starved to death. Klaus won't be back.

Bathers have no business to come down to the boiler room. The boiler room is a place apart, any coming and going between the pool area and the boiler room is prohibited, since coal dust inevitably sticks to clothes and shoes and makes the pool area dirty. Anybody coming from the boiler room must take off his shoes or wipe them clean with a cloth. If there are people here they should keep to this rule, and I try to do so too, although ever since there has been no boiler man I have been responsible for the boilers and can't avoid coming and going between the basement and the pool area.

On no account may the lifeguard sleep in the pool area. If I lie down for a rest, it has to be right in the pool, because as long as I'm lying there no one else will drown. I hear people passing to the right and left of me, sense the movement of the air, the soft footsteps, I hear their whispering, and when I call out they take fright and are gone.

The boiler room, on the other hand, is a deserted place,

I too remain completely silent there, I go down to the basement when I'm exhausted, when I'm tired of talking, listen to the fire in the boilers and the hum of the water in the cylinders and pipes. Even when it's hard for me to keep silent I wait until I'm up in the pool hall again. As a child I used to talk to myself, but that doesn't mean that I'm mad. The sentences bore their way into my mind, one after another, and I walk along the narrow, low-ceilinged passage, up the stairs into the pool area, and before I enter it I wipe my shoes with a cloth.

This is the sixth day that I've been here without having left the building a single time. For the third time a piece of plaster has broken out of the wall.

A little while ago I stoked both the boilers. The coal is nearly all gone. Then I went upstairs to the pool hall and up to the gallery to look out of the window.

I'm not certain whether it's still January or already February. The clock has stopped. The day after the second slab of plaster broke away from the wall, leaving a deep gash exposing rusty iron struts, the clock stopped. Do you hear me? Time has stopped going, movements have no direction even though I take care always to walk around the pool the same way—clockwise. There isn't any calling any more, or splashing, or children's shrieking, only the sentences are still there, as though they were written up on the notices and warning signs. It's very quiet.

Ultimately there'll be nothing left to decay.

I've put the tile back in its place, and I know that it's loose. For the fish I've bought fish food, and I've brought a duster and a cloth from my mother's flat to wipe the globes with. For the first few weeks I kept food under the table in the tool room; there are tins of fruit and several packets of crispbread. Soon I shall have used it all up. At the start I used the kettle to make tea for myself. When the fish food has all gone the catfish will die. They're still swimming up and down, just as I walk around the pool, but their movements are slowing down, and I'm weary too.

The smell is getting stronger again. The foul smell in the basement. The dead fish. The catfish. Klaus scooped some water for the catfish out of the swimming pool before it was drained. If no one else is going to be swimming in that water, at least the fish can, he said, and he filled a bucket with water and emptied it into the aquarium. But I had to change the water. There's none of the swimming-pool water left.

The smell is still there, it's growing stronger; the smell of every movement, every grin, every baseness, a whole night, a chance touch, the smell of death, nothing but wasted life, a petty loss: every smell lingering in the water, particles shed by people's bodies, and it's all preserved by the water, the water and the floor-tiles that countless bare feet have walked on, clinging to the tiles and the walls is the smell of those who come, stay briefly, leave again, it was three thousand a week at the beginning, for almost a hundred years, the People's Baths had just opened, there were swimming competitions and displays, and up in the gallery they're still sitting and applauding, a few more weeks or a few more days and that will be all.

Do you hear me? The people can be sent away. There were bathers here every day and now no one comes, the water has gone, everything as quiet as if it had always been like this. The smell wasn't noticeable because chlorine has a stronger smell than anything else, the water smells of chlorine, but you can tell that people have been in the water, and once when the pool was closed for three days and no bathers were allowed in it the water seemed alien to me. I didn't even fancy dipping my hand in. I no longer like being in the pool area. Are you listening to me? Perhaps there is no microphone.

In the basement there are the globes. The third globe is flickering, and two have already gone out. I know I could just go out and buy some new bulbs. Sometimes I stumble as I walk round the pool. I never used to stumble. Soon I shall forget that, just as for a while I had forgotten the others, Frau Karpfe, the caretaker, Klaus, even mother, Cremer and his daughter, and the swimming pool will lie there before my eyes, empty.

For a time everything went on in an orderly fashion. I came back here. The catfish hadn't died. I found my globe, and three more to go with it. If I hadn't kept the boilers going the pipes would have burst. Something remains of the people, in the whole building, on the walls; their breath, a chance touch of the hand, laughter, a call, a gesture. A building deteriorates when there's no one in it. No one can blame me. They are leaving it to decay. But everything will be lost even before that. Not even decay will be left.

Chapter seven

I t's getting colder.

Outside it's just starting to get light. By this evening I shall have used up the last of the coal. I've put the two globes that have gone out in the tool room, the other two flank the aquarium, standing on its right and left, the aquarium in which the catfish are swimming to and fro very slowly, their whiskers trailing on the bottom.

Last night I lay down to sleep without getting undressed. I have no clean change of clothes and I shan't shave any more. Last night I also thought of dropping in on Cremer at his kiosk: he would know how I could get my flat opened. He helped me when my mother died some weeks ago. She was put into a coffin in the flat, and Cremer shook his head over the fact that afterwards the urn would be buried without a name. The fish were left here by Klaus. One of the fish was very light because it dried out, it's lying in the swimming pool, roughly at the divide between the non-swimmers' and the swimmers' sections.

Cremer wouldn't recognize me. The shirts and my jacket

are black with coal dust, when I touch my face it's rough and bony, and I've grown a beard. Even dead people's hair goes on growing. If you put flocculent into the water, the hairs combine to form little clumps. Good morning, Hugo, Cremer used to say in the mornings, but now I have no name. Some homeless person, he'd think, and I'd go on my way. I shan't do any more wandering around the city, my leather shoes are all scuffed, even the soles of my trainers are worn thin. I'm not going to go along the corridor to the entrance hall and past the mirrors.

I am the lifeguard. I've never been one to say much. The coal is nearly all gone, one boiler has already gone out, and it won't be long now before the fire goes out in the second one, today, this evening. It already feels chillier.

Just now I thought there was someone knocking at the door.

I had just seen that there wasn't enough coal left for the second boiler. I'd decided to let everything take its course, and that I wouldn't go up into the pool hall any more.

In the basement it's dark. The room is lit only by the bluish light of the globes, the light of two globes. Two have gone out, and the third globe is flickering. Some dim, half-light comes in through the panes of milky glass, the sky is overcast, an oppressive, dark morning as though there'll be no more days. And it's sure to be cold. It *is* cold, because it's winter, still winter. The winter is never-ending. If it would only get warmer the damage could be held in check. The damp is getting into the walls; they're starting to develop mould. The People's Baths should be closed down, they said, because the building is falling into decay. They are letting it decay. That was their plan from the very start.

A slab of plaster broke away from the wall and, as on the first occasion, it came from directly above a pillar. That aroused my suspicions. I suspected that someone might have followed me, that someone was watching me, listening to me. It was no coincidence that the first time it happened it wasn't me in the pool hall but the caretaker, who quickly fetched a shovel and broom and swept up the larger pieces of debris before calling the others. He had something to hide. I had been in the basement boiler room, the pool area had been empty. He had been waiting for that moment. Perhaps he wanted to hide the microphones. The closure of the whole Baths has made that unnecessary.

When a second piece broke away from the wall I became suspicious. Above the pillars the paint is a slightly different color. I am being watched, listened to. Who knows what may be concealed in the wall, beneath the plaster. In among the rusting struts I could make out a tangle of black wires. The walls were built of stone or brick, so I had believed, the People's Baths, a building that could never be damaged, whoever might come and go there, whoever might be the manager, the caretaker, the lifeguard, it made no difference. But all of that was an illusion, the massive arches like those in a church, the vaulting, the high barrel-vaulted ceiling space in which voices resonate. It's nothing but metal struts and mortar covered with plaster, and it's easy to conceal microphones there.

They were never well disposed towards me, neither the caretaker nor Frau Karpfe, the others said nothing but sometimes I heard how they talked behind my back: a man who lives with his mother and voluntarily does the work of two, retarded, they said, an idiot, a crackpot. I said nothing, I was never one to talk much. Years ago two men came, wanted me to pay attention to what the bathers talked about, to eavesdrop when they spoke. I was to report back to them on who the people were, what their names were. I never talked much and never listened to anybody, I didn't know the bathers, didn't know their names. I took care to keep it that way and only listened when someone called for help. I learned nothing either about the bathers or about anyone else, not even about my father. He hanged himself. Whatever I might have said wouldn't have influenced the decision. The decisions were already taken. Think yourself lucky that we let you learn a trade at all. I never talked much, first I was the lifeguard's assistant, then I was the lifeguard myself, that's all there was to it. I had no need to take a decision, I wasn't asked, and later I said nothing. No one drowned.

I came back here. Although I entered without authority, it can't be called a break-in. The key was given to me by the caretaker. I've been here for several weeks now. It was only when a second piece of plaster broke away from the wall, a week ago, that my suspicions were aroused. What is it that you want to hear from me? An attempt was made years ago to pump me for information. He's an informer, Klaus had said, pointing to the caretaker. I sometimes think I see him, he walks very softly, rather hurriedly, he has a reddish face and above his broad nose you can hardly see his little blue eyes. Whenever Frau Karpfe summoned me to her office, she would shine her reading lamp straight in my face. I would look away though I never had anything to hide, and even if people follow me and eavesdrop on me they won't find anything to accuse me of.

    I saved the fish; I got rid of the stench of the dead ones and prevented the water pipes from bursting. There could easily have been a flood, water would have poured right out on to the street, completely flooded the pool and the basement and the narrow passages linking the pool area and the boiler room. It would have been discovered too late. The corpses and the stench of them would have polluted the street and the city. These are the People's Baths, and no one knows them as well as I do. Every morning the surface of the water appeared smooth and untouched. After that the bathers came, disturbed the water, and you couldn't see anything. But something of their bodies stays behind in the water, a faint smell, and unless you're very familiar with it you don't notice it for the smell of the chlorine. A faint smell that clings to the walls, minute particles which all the people have left behind, day in, day out, without knowing it.

One boiler is already cold, the other will go out soon, and I never used the third one. When there's no water there's no need to heat it. I didn't sleep last night. The fish continue to swim backwards and forwards, pausing for a moment when the globe flickers. The two other globes are standing there as dark as if no day would ever dawn again. Last night I lay awake on the old camp bed, which I've moved into the big room because I can't stand the small one. I no longer switch the light on, except for the light in the washroom, which has no windows. I haven't shaved for days. Not even Cremer would recognize me.

When I came back here I took charge of everything, spent the daytime up in the pool area and went down to the basement to feed the fish, stoke the boilers. And when it was dark I went out to buy food for myself and fish food, and I also bought adhesive for the tile that had come loose. Just at first I went back to the flat to sleep, then I brought a blanket here and the clothes that I needed. It can't be called a break-in. The flat is sealed up now, I'm regarded as having disappeared, and I can't go back there again. No one can blame me. I had the key to the side entrance, and my old globe was in the boiler room. The names and the borders are wrong. But the globe clearly shows that two thirds of the earth consists of water. I was deliberately ordered to let out the water. The swimming pool is closed and the individual baths aren't in use any more either. A slab of plaster came away from the wall. I no longer believe it was a coincidence. Six days ago it happened again, a slab of plaster immediately above one of the pillars, just like the first time when I wasn't in the pool hall and the caretaker quickly swept up the larger pieces of debris which had fallen next to the pool, and in among the mortar and the iron struts you can make out black wires. I believed that the building was solidly built, of stone or brick, but it's not true.

When it happened for the second time I swept up the mess, and without thinking I took it downstairs and emptied the metal bucket into the boiler.

"An informer," Klaus said, pointing to the caretaker. Years ago an attempt was made to interrogate me. But they can't threaten me. I never wanted to be a lifeguard.

I used to read at night by the light of the globe so that no one would notice.

"Didn't you want to go to university?" they asked derisively. They also asked about my father, and later about the old lifeguard.

"What did you see?"

I said nothing. I've never talked much, and when they wanted me to eavesdrop on the bathers I didn't answer.

The borders are wrong, the names are wrong. Do you hear me? The books have long since gone, the globe too, now the flat is standing empty and my mother is dead. I always lived there, my father hanged himself there, he had his reasons, he was merely the last of the dead in his own life, the others were shot, there were photographs, so we were told, and my mother emptied boxes, collected together the things she wanted me to take down for the dustmen and put them by the door, just as she had put the globe by the door.

"The borders are wrong," she declared. My books had gone before that.

"You don't need them," she told me. I only slept in the flat, nothing more, now it's been sealed up by the police and I'm not going back there.

Nothing but decay, a building that's falling apart,

abandoned as though no one had ever been here. Do you hear me? The sentences, the sentences on the warning notices are finally disappearing. Only my voice is still here, and sometimes I ask myself where it's coming from, because it's very quiet here, and I've never been one to talk much.

I see the gaping holes in the walls, see the cracks in the colors; they remind me of the old bathers who used to come early in the morning, and of their pale skin, the blue veins, the liver spots, and when you look away you still see the feet, with their yellowish deformed nails serving no purpose but to carry on growing after death. Ugliness lasts longer than life. From the very first day I hated it, from that day when I was under instructions to report at the pool hall at 7a.m. It was winter, with the water hardly visible in the dimness of the emergency lighting; when the lifeguard came up to me it startled me.

Seven o'clock, I knew what to bring, they ordered, and so I set off as if I were going swimming. Stood by the empty pool, waited, a caretaker had let me in, but the pool hall was empty, the water unruffled. It would only be for a short time, I thought; it's a mistake, I wanted to say to the lifeguard when he came, but he eyed me with obvious distrust, so I said nothing. I wouldn't recognize him now, this was forty years ago. I only remember that he was taller than me and asked if I hadn't got a bathrobe. I hadn't, I had to ask my mother for one, she wouldn't hear of it, her own son couldn't possibly be a lifeguard, she declared, and refused to buy me a bathrobe. After two weeks the old lifeguard gave me his old one, which was gray from repeated washing, and which I wore for a long time. Three years later, when I was still a lifeguard and had been the only one for a considerable time, I found on coming home one evening that my books had been put into boxes and my mother was standing in my room.

"You don't need the books, they only collect dust," my

mother said, fetching a carrier bag from her bedroom. "Those books need to be got rid of," she added, and demanded that I take them downstairs. I carried the boxes, four boxes, down into the courtyard. What happened to them after that I don't know. When I came back up, there, lying on my bed was the new bathrobe.

For a year I was the assistant. The lifeguard stood on one side of the swimming pool and I stood on the other.

Three times I was summoned for a meeting: I thought I was going to be told that now I could go to university. But they wanted to know whether I was happy with the job, whether the lifeguard treated me well. You can probably learn a thing or two from him, they said, and told me to write a report about my work. What did I know about the lifeguard, I was asked. Do you hear me? That was forty years ago. I wouldn't recognize him now, and even then I knew nothing about him beyond the fact that he was the lifeguard. They had put him to work in the Swimming Baths because he lived next door and because the former lifeguard, his predecessor, had been his uncle. Of what took place in the Swimming Baths he knew nothing until the war was over, he said. He had to help carry them out, they were already dead by then. He spoke little, even to me, and then only in the evenings, just before we went home.

As always he was standing on the one side and I was opposite him, the pool area was already empty, I didn't know what they had come for, it was two men, he knew them, wasn't surprised. I saw him standing there with the net in his hand, he was very thin and was standing bent forward as though leaning on a stick when they ordered him to go with them. It was only then that they saw me, and they were angry and told me to stay where I was. It happened very fast. He refused to obey, and when they started to move towards him he fell down on to the tiles. Then they dragged him away.

Three days later, when I left at the end of the day, they were waiting for me in front of the People's Baths. They ordered me to get into their car. I can't remember the lifeguard. They showed me photographs and claimed that my father appeared in them, but I didn't recognize him. Had I seen what had happened to the lifeguard? they asked. I had seen it. I've forgotten it. Now no one comes here any more, and no one saw what happened. I said nothing.

I took the floor cloth and his bathrobe to the dustbins. Did you know him, the two men asked me, mockingly. Did you burn his clothes, maybe? I suppose you were after his job?

Can you hear me out there? I haven't spoken about this to anyone. "A strange choice of profession, being a lifeguard," they sneered, and what did my mother have to say about that, was I completely devoid of ambition?

"It was high time," one of them told me when they were about to drop me off near the flat, "that this swimming pool had a lifeguard again. There might easily have been an accident," he said. Just imagine if someone had drowned. "You don't want that to happen, do you?"

No one drowned. Do you hear? The bathrobe was stained, and so were the tiles. Everyone had left long before, the Swimming Baths had already closed for the day, and the caretaker and the manager had gone too; I was the only other person still there, the lifeguard had kept me behind. He had told me to stay on, it was time I learned how to chlorinate the water in the evening, I would soon have to do it myself. The very next day I became the lifeguard, as if there had never been any other. Not long after that a new caretaker Frau Karpfe came, and it was like it was all just a rumor.

The two men asked me if I remembered.

"But remember what?"
One of them said: "What is there to remember?"

Later, it went around that a child had drowned while he was on duty, or that he had simply cleared off. I knew nothing about it. They had the keys; they took him down into the boiler room and out through the side entrance while I stayed in the pool hall, waiting, waiting, until the two of them came back and one of them swore at me, asking why I hadn't wiped up the blood. There were only a few drops, on the spot where the lifeguard had fallen down. He'd probably had a nosebleed, which can happen. Then they sent me down to the boiler room and ordered me to put the bathrobe and the floor cloth in the dustbins, unlocked the iron door to the back yard, and I went home.

I stood alone at the edge of the pool. You only need to scoop up a little water out of the pool in order to wash off marks and dirt, you bend or squat down at the side of the pool, dip your hands into the water; that's all. You splash some water over the tiles with your hands. You don't have to go and fetch water specially, and you don't need a bucket. A cloth will do, and you can easily rinse it in the pool. The water looks no different, the water is always just as it was before, no trace remains behind unless you know otherwise; anyhow, there's always the same smell of chlorine. A great deal depends on the quality of the water. The bathers got undressed and swam as usual. They noticed nothing, climbed out of the water as normal, you couldn't see anything different about them and they themselves saw nothing. There was nothing to see, and I said nothing. That evening, I got home late, switched on the light of the globe and got into bed and said nothing, and my mother didn't ask. I had hated the baths from the very first day, had stood at the side of the pool for a year as an assistant without saying a word. Now I was the lifeguard.

I attended scrupulously to the quality of the water, but I ran out of chlorine and flocculent, and when the authorities sent an inspector he found it unsatisfactory.

None of the bathers asked after the old lifeguard. They saw me at the side of the pool, saw that I was alone and said nothing, and the caretaker and the manager didn't ask either. Then they were transferred, a new caretaker and Frau Karpfe came, and everything went on as before, as if not the smallest incident had ever occurred, as if there had never been a different lifeguard before me. I said nothing; when they were waiting for me outside the Baths, three days later, I had nothing to hide. What is there for him to remember? the second one asked, and showed me a photograph: after all, he was still only a child. And there were children in the photograph, lying piled up in a pit, at the edge of which stood a man who resembled my father.

I had seen nothing, no one had drowned, there was no blood on the tiles, and I carried the bathrobe out to the dustbins.

This shirt has stains on it. Just now I thought I saw myself reflected in the water, I saw the stained shirt, the unshaven chin. An old man, shabby and unkempt. For a moment, as I bent over the empty pool, I seemed to see water and my reflection: the sort of man who lives on the streets and talks to himself. Not even Cremer would recognize me.

I was incapable, they thought.

"Retarded," they whispered behind my back, "simple-minded, unable to do anything but parrot the words on the notices around the pool." *Face towards the ladder!*

Now I'm waiting. The pool is full of water again, they come first thing in the morning, call out a good morning to me, disappear into the changing rooms, come into the pool area in their bathing things and stand at the edge of the pool, bend down, stretch out a hand as though to feel the temperature of the water, then stop moving. The old woman with her sparse white hair stands by the steps, even thinner than before, her right knee swollen, a man of about forty reaches for the ladder, two scars standing out vividly on his big, dark back, the fat woman with her grandchild stays behind a pillar, holding the child's arm tightly. They all seem turned to stone, they've only just come in, the pool was filled to the brim, they seem not to recognize me, then they turn away, the pool lies there empty and dusty, and they leave, I can't prevent them. I wanted to call out, it was just a minute ago, wanted to call out, but nobody hears me.

I hated them, the bathers. The naked girls day after day, you can't fool me, the old lifeguard went into the women's changing room, we stood opposite each other, he on the one side, I on the other, he where the women got undressed, I on the men's side; he paid no attention to the pool and the swimmers, stood with his back to the water and to me, an old man, he would constantly find some job to do in the changing room and near the showers, I watched him for a year, watched him and the way he helped young women out of the water, how he would give them a pat, his old body, blotchy, flabby, a tall man, the women didn't seem to object, an old man turning to look at every girl, eyeing their legs, their breasts, and there'd be an accidental pat on a bottom, a hand on a shoulder, a seemingly-innocent brushing by in passing or by way of assistance. His flabby body was similar to the hanged body of my father, he had taken his shirt off just as he always ordered me to take my shirt off before he beat me, weals on my back, he only stopped beating me when I took up swimming and the others could see my back. Later I stopped swimming. The old lifeguard could still make me, he used to jump in himself and I had to haul him out, putting my arms around his chest and gripping him firmly, I had to swim every day, the chlorine eats away at your skin and bleaches your hair, in the evenings he would insist on my staying on longer, would sit down on the wooden bench and start talking, to me or to himself, and as he sat there his body was as flabby and limp as that of my hanged father.

For years I didn't think about it, didn't want to think about it; I was the lifeguard. I didn't speak more than was absolutely necessary, and now the words are like the dust on the tiles, you can't breathe. For days I've been walking up and down here, I can't get it out of my mind, all those years as empty as the pool, and I know that the tiles are coming loose. They wouldn't hold the water in any more, time is congealing, you need to wash it away, to drown time, this is unbearable, they don't come any more, you just have to scoop some water out of the pool and then the stains are gone and nothing has happened.

This is the last day. Light filters through the panes as feebly as if it were trying to make the color of the tiles fade away. Once they shone green and blue, on some evenings the flowers on the pillars sparkled like jewels in a banqueting hall, the fish on the iron banisters seemed alive, as if they were about to go swimming off in the water, and Tanja, Cremer's daughter, asked me why I didn't let them into the pool. In the middle of the pool a dead fish is lying, it's very light, dried out, I carried it there with my own hands, now it's only a small dark patch, you can't make it out unless you know it's there, it's always like that with dead bodies, after a short time you can't see them any more. Tanja, too, was very light when I picked her up because Cremer's hands were shaking. I'm not to blame for her death. She would be grown up now, she wouldn't be coming here any more, and if nothing had happened to him that time the old lifeguard would be dead now just the same. No one comes here any more. The colors are growing dull, and where faces used to be reflected when they leaned over the water there's only dust now. Dust is what's left in the end, it covers the tiles, and in the aquarium the fish swim slowly as if the dust were about to suffocate them.

The paw of the end lion has broken off, as though the stone had grown tired. I don't know why this reminds me of the old lifeguard. Why they came to get him I don't know. He didn't want any bother with anybody, he said, but I didn't know who it was he meant. The men were angry when they saw me. I never wanted to be here, I would have been glad to leave.

Now it's too late. It must be midday, I could go out and call at Cremer's kiosk, he's sure to be open again, selling rolls. If I don't speak the silence is unbearable, I don't even hear the mice and rats any more. The bats have disappeared, or else I was mistaken and it wasn't the bats I saw, those thin shadows flitting through the pool area, coming to rest up in the gallery. Or perhaps it's too cold for them, it's getting colder by the hour. Just now I went down the first few steps leading into the shallow end, two loose tiles rattled under my feet, I bent down, in the dust there's human hair and above the dust the smell of chlorine and sweat. They haven't gone, the bathers are still here even though everything has been cleared out, even though the caretaker and Frau Karpfe have long since locked the place up and there's a notice posted up at the entrance:

The swimming pool is closed.

At the start I expected that a new lifeguard would come any day and I'd be able to leave. The caretaker and the manager were transferred elsewhere, Frau Karpfe came into the pool hall and greeted me as if I were the main lifeguard.

The years were all the same. I know the Swimming Baths better than anyone else. Nothing has ever happened. I taught

Tanja, Cremer's daughter, to swim, and she didn't drown. If she had come here on that last day, the lorry wouldn't have run her over. When I used to leave the Swimming Baths at eight o'clock Cremer would be packing up his newspapers, I would take Tanja to him and we'd wait together until Cremer had locked up the kiosk. But on that day Tanja hadn't come, and as I came along the street I saw her playing on the pavement in front of the kiosk. Then she saw me, started to run around the kiosk, and behind the kiosk she jumped out into the road. Cremer saw nothing, I saw the lorry and then Cremer heard me. Why hadn't I noted the registration number, I was asked. I called out very loudly. The lorry was reversing, turning into the side street, and Tanja ran into the road. I taught Tanja to swim. For three years she came almost every day and played and swam here. She was a very good swimmer, she would never have drowned, and there was no need to worry about her.

For a time I kept two bathing costumes belonging to Tanja. Then I gave them to the boiler man to put with the lost property. They may still be in the cupboard. They weren't needed. No one asked what became of them, I didn't either, and I didn't look for them, only for the globe, which I took out of the cupboard and put in the boiler room. My old globe has stopped working, the bulb has gone, a third globe is flickering, and here and there there's a thin shaft of white light piercing a continent or a sea, as harsh as Frau Karpfe's reading lamp. It's been seven days now. Everything that I could say, I have said. The pool hall, the pool, the whole building is going to collapse. Perhaps it will soon be demolished. Can anyone hear what I'm saying?

It was the water.

The water belonged to me. Now there's a layer of dust on the tiles, and every step leaves a visible print. This morning I thought someone was knocking. It must be afternoon now.

Do you hear me? I stand at the edge of the pool in front of the pillars, or under the gallery, above me the grimacing lion heads. The clock has stopped. On the steps going down into the shallow end I found hairs. They say that people's hair and fingernails go on growing after death. The people have disappeared of their own accord, it doesn't take death to make them disappear. The bathers who came here have gone, as though they had never existed, and now that the pool is empty, the pool hall closed, there's no lifeguard any more. One decision, one letter was all it took to bring the whole thing to an end. I couldn't believe it. I came back here. The building, the walls, the pool hall and the tiles are still here. Where am I to go? I've spent all these years here. Its forty years now. I didn't ask to do that. The pool drained, the pool hall and the whole baths closed down, just a decision, a letter saying that my services are no longer required. They can't do this to me. Where am I to go?

The days are long. Time doesn't pass any more, but that doesn't halt the decay. I have come back here. They have laid the responsibility for time on me. Someone has to keep hold of time, each day, the weeks, someone has to keep an eye on time like a clock to prevent everything from decaying, disappearing, just as someone looks after the water, adds chlorine, cleans the filters and takes pains to ensure that nothing pollutes the water. No one apart from me knows the exact composition of the water. A glance at any bather, any swimmer, tells me how much chlorine and how much flocculent needs to be added to the water, you can judge it by their faces and their skin and the degree of their tiredness and their expressions; each day is different. Something is left behind in the water, something of each individual. Since the water has been let out, the years that I have spent here count for nothing. The baths have been closed and I've been sent packing. Now it's too late. I'm not going out any more, nor am I going down into the basement. It's already getting chillier, and tomorrow it will be cold, so cold that the last vestige of warmth in the walls will be lost and the pipes will burst.

There's no going back.

This year the days aren't growing longer. From the windows of the gallery you can look out and see the trees in the street. The bare branches hang in the air like cracks in the windowpanes, it's only when you move your head that you realize there are branches and twigs outside. I'm not going up into the gallery any more. The air has a crack in it. Perhaps they have made the bathers form up in a long line outside. The bathers are waiting in the cold, soon they'll freeze to death. There's no going back. They're still breathing but their breathing is labored, there's dust hanging in the air. The dust is poisonous. Two tiles on the steps have come loose, I've removed them and put them down on the side, they lie there looking dull and rattle if your foot touches them. They hardly weigh anything when you pick them up, they're shrinking and cracks are appearing. Soon the other tiles will become detached too, and when you walk into the empty pool your footsteps will clatter as if you were walking through shards of broken pottery. I've taken my shoes off so that no one can hear me. It's already cold. Tanja had caught a cold too, from running around barefoot, and her mother didn't let her go to the Swimming Baths. She hadn't taken her shoes off near Cremer's kiosk. You don't take your shoes off in the street. The skin cracks, the sore places refuse to heal. Do you hear me? The bathers will catch cold. You shouldn't go into the water with a temperature. Someone ought to help them. They've been waiting outside for weeks now. The clock has stopped, it happened quite some time ago. The lions which have always held up the gallery have lost a paw, and perhaps there are no shadows, perhaps there's only dust. I bent down to look. I wanted to collect up the dust. But the shadows are afraid; even dead people are afraid. As far as I'm concerned they're welcome to come here. The Swimming Baths are closed, there's plenty of room. I've taken my shoes off. I don't know whether the dead wear shoes. In the basement it's dirty, my white trainers are covered with dirty marks, I mustn't put them on any more, Frau Karpfe and the caretaker would report me, they'd have good reason to dismiss me. A few years ago they threatened to do just that, and said I wouldn't find another job, I was the lifeguard, I'd never learned any other trade, no one would give me a job, they said. Now I'd be able to go to university, the caretaker scoffed. I don't know who told him about that, and it's mean. Perhaps I should go to the flat and fetch my bathrobe. Even if I'm regarded as having disappeared and the door is sealed up, no one will try to stop me from collecting my bathrobe. The lifeguard has to have a bathrobe.

I've come back here. There was nowhere else. I'm not going down to the basement, I don't need the bed any more, don't want to sleep. If I fall asleep I shan't wake up again. The fish are swimming slowly now. I'm afraid to look at them. They are fishes of death, I knew that from the start. They have whiskers that trail on the bottom of the aquarium.

Perhaps Tanja will come, perhaps she'll knock or call my name. But I can't let her in to show her the globe. In the narrow passage between the basement and the side entrance there's a smell of death. They drove the bathers in there. Their cries could be heard from outside, then everything went quiet. No one passing the building even turns his head.

The fish were left here by Klaus, the small fish died of starvation, the aquarium stank and was nothing but a black box. I was going to clean it out, but it slipped from my hands and broke. But Klaus hasn't come back, no one has asked about it, and now the catfish will die too. They swim slowly to and fro, just as I have walked up and down beside the empty pool. If someone is here the building won't decay, so I thought, but a second and a third slab of plaster have broken away from the wall, the walls won't hold, and in the end they'll be demolished. I'm tired. Do you hear me? It's impossible to collect up the dust; it slips through your hands just like water, and it's getting thicker and thicker, it already covers the tiles, dust where there used to be water, I found a hair and I've run out of flocculent. I can't do anything about it. Where the stairs lead up to the gallery there were always cobwebs. But now they completely conceal the stairway, and the web is black and thick. When even I am no longer here the cobwebs will spread still more. It's not a place for human beings. I was the one who let the water out, the pool has been empty for months, everything that could be removed from the building has gone, the caretaker even took one bench, I listed it myself on the file cards that Frau Karpfe gave me. For two weeks I went on working, looking after the individual baths, but hardly anyone came. Next to the bath cubicles there's a vestibule, I sat and waited there until one day the letter came telling me that I had to go. I signed a paper myself saying that I was willing to take early retirement. I'd thought the baths would never be closed, that the letter the manageress told me to sign was one opposing the closure of the People's Baths. If I signed she would order chlorine and flocculent within two days, so she said. The water wasn't in good condition, and I'd never been ill, there was no reason for me to be pensioned off early.

The caretaker scoffed at me: "Do you know now what it was you signed?"

It was evening; I left as usual, without saying a word to Cremer, nor to my mother.

A slab of plaster broke away from the wall. We all gathered in the office, in the evening everybody went to a pub. I believed that everything was about to change, and I thought people wouldn't stand by and let the People's Baths be closed. But that was a mistake. I was wrong. On the fifth day the others went without me, leaving me behind in the Swimming Baths. They wanted it to be closed. That was clearly their intention from the start.

No one said anything. It was a day like any other. That day they took mortar out of the wall. Time waits in the walls, waits with decay. Every day since the Swimming Baths first opened is preserved here as if it were built into the wall, time itself and the smell of every bather who has ever been here, tiny particles that allow nothing to be forgotten. I should have known that. The chlorine in the water has to disguise it, the water itself does nothing but dilute those traces to make them bearable. The bodies are only the residue of all that has happened, all the ugliness, the hasty movements, the weariness and finally death, and only the water keeps going back to being smooth and calm, as though nothing had ever happened, as though nothing were too ugly to be reflected in it. It's very peaceful. Each morning that peacefulness is there again, the light comes in through the windows, and the water is there waiting: the days pass by, one after another, there's no need to be afraid of them.

But they have let the water out; I myself opened the outflow.

They deliberately broke a hole in the wall. Perhaps it was the caretaker. He's a heavily built man, he could raise his hand and kill someone. Perhaps they engineered the whole thing, he and Frau Karpfe. They're hand-in-glove, informers—that's what Klaus, the boiler man, called them. They were always trying to taunt and make fun of me. As long as the water was here there was nothing they could do to me.

A short while ago I went down the steps into the shallow end of the pool, where some tiles are loose, showing gray beneath the dust. There ought to be water there, even if it does slip through your hands like dust, there's no such thing as a pool without water. I was mistaken.

I came back here, the lifeguard has to see to it that no one drowns, and no one has ever drowned while I've been here; I walk up and down beside the pool, I don't sleep, you have to keep your eyes open, and if you're quick to notice the first signs, simply calling out quite gently is enough to avert disaster, and often just saying aloud what is written on the warning notices will do:

No jumping in from the sides! Face towards the pool steps!

I was never ill, I never missed a day. Everything depends on averting disaster, and the water should never have been let out. It's easier to change the Earth than a globe. If it weren't for the dead fish lying there I could put the four globes into the pool. They float on the water looking like heads, and when a bather swims past they rock gently as if they were being rocked to sleep. My head ought to be among them, it's quite easy once the decision has been taken, then it soaks up water, most objects sink, the lifeguard has to watch out for that, otherwise they sink to the bottom and are never found again, and since the water has been let out a lot of people have already disappeared from here, I'd been sent packing, for some weeks I wasn't at my post, I should never have gone away. It was wrong. Perhaps Cremer is here too, folding the newspapers into little boats to please Tanja, the dead are supposed to cross over in boats, they have coins in their mouths to pay for the crossing, but the pool is too small, a boat has no business to be in a swimming pool, and the opposite bank is very far away, they'll never get there however hard they try.

It hadn't occurred to me to close the outlet valve again. It's a big iron sliding valve secured by a hook, and it yielded without any resistance, just as I obeyed the instruction without a word of objection, heard the water, heard it flowing away. The water level is falling, I can see it before me, the tiles on the sides are still covered with droplets, water is trickling down them, it's dwindling, I shouldn't have done it, shouldn't have opened the valve, only a couple of movements, just one hand taking hold of the handle, I didn't utter a single word of protest, the mocking face of the caretaker before me, the tiles round the sides are glistening with moisture, soon the pool will be half empty, there'd still be time to stop it happening, and even when it's quite empty one might still think that it's only going to be cleaned, the old water replaced by new, replaced by fresh water once the tiles and joints have been thoroughly scoured and any damage made good. The lifeguard is responsible for that, he's the only one who can assess the quality of the water, and no step may be taken without his agreement.

The pipes are getting cold, they're contracting, I can tell that from the knocking sound the metal makes, it's as if someone were trying to signal to me. No, there wasn't a knock at the main entrance door. Just now I went up to the gallery again to look out at the street, I thought that surely someone must be coming. Haven't you heard what I've been saying? It was a mistake. The Swimming Baths mustn't be closed down. Two thirds of the Earth's surface is covered by water, and even if the borders on the globe are wrong now, that doesn't alter the fact. I have four globes, they're in the basement. They would float on the water. There's still some food in the basement, too, tinned food and potatoes, I needn't die of starvation even if I don't go back to the flat, I won't be driven away a second time, and in the aquarium the fish are swimming, swimming slowly. Klaus claimed that he ate them. No one ever came to harm while I was here, no bather drowned in all those years, they have swimming trunks and costumes on, they're not naked, and dead people have a full set of clothes put on them even if they're being cremated. You can't confuse the dead and the living. But it's not all that important, and anyone who wants to swim here is welcome. The swimming pool is all mine now. The others haven't got the necessary knowledge. Not one of them has come back here, and now the day's over, it's getting cold, and by tomorrow the water may have frozen. I don't know what became of the old lifeguard, he fell, I wiped up the blood, took the cloths to the dustbin, and the dustbins are big, big enough for my mother's bedding and much else besides. For days no one has spoken here, no one says good morning to me, Cremer hasn't come looking for me and Klaus hasn't come back to feed his fish, the small fish have died, they stink, the evil smell mingles with the years, and if the pipes burst then everything will be flooded with sewage water. I've seen rats, they live in the drains, they carry the stench from place to place, perhaps they feed on dead people, perhaps that's why those shadowy figures look for a place up in the gallery.

Who knows what there is in the walls. They're not built of stone. Perhaps it's only straw and plaster. I believed that the Swimming Baths couldn't decay. Perhaps they want them to decay so that no one finds out what's concealed in the walls. When the first lump of plaster broke away from the wall the caretaker was in the pool area and swept up the bigger pieces of debris himself. That should have aroused my suspicions. They were probably in a hurry to get away, and they took with them anything that seemed usable. Frau Karpfe spent days in her office clearing out the cupboards. I don't know what there was in her office, I haven't been in there since I've been back. She informed me that I was dismissed; there were papers on the desk in front of her, and behind me stood the caretaker. The lamp is dazzling me, you've no reason to interrogate me. Perhaps no one is listening to me? Why does nobody come to arrest me? In her office Frau Karpfe had a small wall cupboard which was never open.

"They record what we say in here," Klaus whispered to me. He left the fish here although he knew they would starve to death. Perhaps he was lying to me? It's so quiet, the heating pipes are knocking, I can't hear my own voice any more, the floor tiles are cold, the tiles in the pool create an illusion, no water, in the dust I can see footprints, there are more and more of them, as though they were all assembling here, children's feet, men, women, the wearing of shoes is prohibited, my father's cellar was full of shoes, they kicked the old lifeguard, I wiped up the blood. Sometimes two people failed to reappear when I wanted to lock up the baths for the night. I would cough and wait for them to emerge from the changing cubicle, embarrassed or laughing, for men are not allowed in the women's changing area. I never condoned such goings-on, and if the caretaker claims that I did he's lying. I stayed behind alone.

The others left and no one came back. But that won't help them, and when the building falls into disrepair their time will be up. The years that they spent here stick to the blue tiles like the dust, and if I fill up the pool again it will be washed away. They didn't take their shoes off, thought they could ignore the rules, laughed at me because I called out the instructions and warnings in a clearly audible voice, but now they're falling off the ladders backwards and crashing down on to the bottom of the pool. Nobody's stopping them. As soon as something has happened it seems as though it had always been like that. The Swimming Baths are closed and no one says a word, people simply pass by, they've got used to it, sometimes I hear sounds but no one answers when I call, no one asks why the light isn't turned on, why the boilers have gone out. The pipes are knocking, soon they'll have gone completely cold. Draped over one pipe are the two towels which I covered myself with on the first night. They have a musty smell and I've spread them out so that they won't go moldy, but the walls are damp too, and if you run your finger over them you feel the thin, slimy layer of mould.

After dark it's eerie in the pool hall. There's no light in there any more. There used to be the emergency lighting, and even when that was switched off the water itself still reflected the faint light of the streetlamps. It was just the night in between two days, that was all. First thing in the morning the bathers came, disappeared into the changing rooms, then showered before coming into the pool area to swim. I knew most of them, their movements and their manner of breathing, how long they swam for and how fast, their measured breathing to begin with, becoming rapid when they had worn themselves out. And although over the years a large number stopped coming, there were always new ones, even in summer when the outdoor pool was open, and many people prefer swimming out of doors in an open-air pool or a lake. An indoor pool can't compare with a lake, and a few years ago the caretaker suggested that the Swimming Baths should be closed during the summer. He made this suggestion to the others in a loud voice, grinning at me.

"We can always leave Hugo here to look after the water."

Then he added in a meaningful undertone, "You can work out at long last what happened to the old lifeguard. What became of him?"

I didn't do anything. He was trying to frighten me. And someone does have to look after the water, otherwise it turns cloudy, someone has to see to it that no one drowns. That's how it's always been, that's how it was before I came. The bathers come, they go quietly into the changing rooms and emerge naked. They stand naked at the edge of the pool. If it's too chilly, they'll catch cold.

The knocking sounds like footsteps, like a person restlessly pacing to and fro. It's gradually growing louder. Perhaps there are people in the other parts of the building, upstairs where the individual baths were, on the stairs themselves or near to the main entrance; it doesn't sound like individual steps going from one specific place to another, the order of things is disrupted, it sounds as if each step were being counted, as if the breaths were being listed, I can hear them, they're growing louder and louder. Frau Karpfe and the caretaker have gone, the others are coming back as though they were hoping to swim here again, as though they missed the swimming, up and down the pool, steadily up and down, and one person is rigorously keeping watch to see that no one sinks and perishes. As you walk you can count the tiles, they are still lying there in orderly rows, as orderly as graves, even if some of them are loose. We've waited a long time, now we're still waiting despite being free to go, we still go up and down, to and fro four times in every hour, five times round the pool in an hour, there are requirements, regulations, no one drowning, the lifeguard isn't falling asleep.

The bathers are coming back. I hated them, naked bodies interminably swimming from one end to the other, their eyes gazing fixedly ahead, no trace left in the water, only a smell remains, even now, on the dusty tiles, and they're coming, all those who have ever been here, as though they could recover something, sandals, a towel, the same time every day, and then another day, the same day all over again.

I must count the tiles. They'll take even the tiles away, like the cupboards and the bench, they're taking take the whole building away and it's better not to sleep.

Perhaps it's best to stay in the pool itself. The tiles taste bitter, but my feet are bare, in accordance with the rules.

The dust tastes bitter. Can you hear me? I'm tired and soon it will be dark, I need to sit down.

It's as quiet as if even the street, the district, the whole city were deserted. Around the edge of the pool there's a strip of granite which holds the tiles in place, but if the pool stays empty it will collapse, the water will flood the building, the basement, the entrance hall, the street, it will cover the whole city, the same dust, the same smell, there isn't enough chlorine to disguise the fact that something of every day and every bather is left behind, just as drops run off the skin when a person gets out of the water. They're standing naked, with heads bowed, and you can't hear a sound even from the children, they're clinging to their parents, their arms, their legs already as tired as if they too had walked every step, to and fro, and the next day as well, in the hope that things will change, just as I waited, just as one waits in order to forget the days, so that it will come to an end at last. They must leave, it's too late.

I also waited. For the mistake to be cleared up, for them to tell me I could leave, and then years go by, then you think everything is about to change, the tiles are drying out and splitting, you can see the fine cracks, do as you're told or suffer the consequences, in the end everything stays the same, the lifeguard disappeared, the bathers are still swimming to and fro, no one's stopping them, and if there's no water they crawl through the dust and wait up in the gallery. I have come back here so that they won't drown, but they're all dead already, their skin dried out, there's a faint rustling sound, and if there were still a fire going in one of the boilers one could burn what's left of them. The lifeguard's clothes are burnt. Now the water gives off a foul smell. A day of calamity, I tried to say, the borders are just a lie, the light flickers for a while longer, then it's all over, it's growing cold, and in the end even the fish will die, will fill their bellies with dust, I'll go down to the basement once more, I've closed off the outflow, now I'm going to open the inlet valve, the fish will stay here, I'll lie down beside them, can't you hear me? I have spoken out loud and clear, the notices are still in place, and those who won't hear must suffer the consequences, I will not wander the city again. Not even Cremer would recognize me. The water in the pool area has been turned off, but the supply for the pool comes from the basement. I knew that all along. My parents' flat is already engulfed by the flood, and if Frau Karpfe and the caretaker come back, then they'll drown and it won't be unintentional. Their only concern was to cover up the fact that they locked us in. Informers, Klaus said, they've installed microphones here, above the pillars. Did I want to take the lifebelt, the caretaker asked me. I haven't swum for years, but no one drowned, and that was my doing. I can prove that people drown when there's no lifeguard here. They can't drive me away. It will be there in the streets for everyone to see, two thirds water, one third land; the globe shows that clearly, the names are irrelevant, I won't be made a fool of any more. First to be flooded will be the platforms, and the passage in the basement; they'll be creeping out of the houses, seeking refuge in the attics, on the roofs, and they will be afraid. This is a day of calamity, but no one heeded the warning. I was driven away: *The Swimming Baths are closed!* Now you'll see where it's got you. Aren't you listening?

The water is eating up the dust. I've brought the fish upstairs in a bucket. They were in a bad state, it was quite easy to catch them. They swim to and fro, just as the bathers did for all those years. But if I empty them out of the bucket they'll thrash about in the shallow water and before the water is deep enough they'll have suffocated. Klaus left them here, the small fish have starved to death. Can you hear me when I'm here in the pool? The water's very cold. Do you hear me? I'm tired now, I need to sit down. All those years I walked to and fro and said not a word. Jumping in from the edge of the pool is prohibited, do you hear? You'll crack your skull, and if you drown no one will help you.

It's already dark. You can't say I didn't warn you. It's seven days now since I last left the baths. The water is rising very slowly. In cold water a person drowns fast. It's already dark, I can't see the fish any more, but the water is up to my ankles, so they won't suffocate. Once the pool is full the water will spread all by itself. At its deepest point the pool is three meters deep.

About the author

Katharina Hacker
Photo by Claus Gretter

Katharina Hacker was born in Frankfurt/Main in 1967. She studied history and Jewish Studies at Freiburg University. In 1990 she continued her studies at the Hebrew University in Jerusalem, where she worked with Saul Friedlander, and at the School for Cultural Studies in Tel Aviv.

The author has resided in Berlin since 1996 where she writes and translates.

The fonts used in the book are from the Garamond and Swiss families